Selected Stories by
LEO TOLSTOY

Books in this Series:

Selected Stories by O. Henry
Selected Stories by Anton Chekhov
Selected Stories by Guy de Maupassant
Selected Stories by Mark Twain
Selected Stories by Edgar Allan Poe
Selected Stories by Rudyard Kipling
Selected Stories by Saki
Selected Stories by Oscar Wilde
Selected Stories by Honoré de Balzac
Selected Stories by Charles Dickens
Selected Stories by D.H. Lawrence
Selected Stories by H.G. Wells
Selected Stories by Jack London
Selected Stories by Joseph Conrad
Selected Stories by Leo Tolstoy
Selected Stories by Sir Arthur Conan Doyle

Selected Stories by
LEO TOLSTOY

Published by
Rupa Publications India Pvt. Ltd 2014
7/16, Ansari Road, Daryaganj
New Delhi 110002

Sales Centres:
Allahabad Bengaluru Chennai
Hyderabad Jaipur Kathmandu
Kolkata Mumbai

Selection and Introduction copyright © Terry O'Brien 2014

All rights reserved.
No part of this publication may be reproduced, transmitted,
or stored in a retrieval system, in any form or by any means,
electronic, mechanical, photocopying, recording or otherwise,
without the prior permission of the publisher.

ISBN: 978-81-291-3149-2

First impression 2014

10 9 8 7 6 5 4 3 2 1

Printed at Shree Maitrey Printech Pvt. Ltd., Noida

This book is sold subject to the condition that it shall not,
by way of trade or otherwise, be lent, resold, hired out, or otherwise
circulated, without the publisher's prior consent, in any form of binding or
cover other than that in which it is published.

CONTENTS

Introduction vii

1. A Candle 1
2. After the Dance 12
3. Albert 24
4. Alyosha the Pot 31
5. An Old Acquaintance 38
6. Does a Man Need Much Land? 68
7. A Spark Neglected Burns the House 85
8. Lucerne 101
9. There are No Guilty People 132
10. God Sees the Truth, but Waits 146

INTRODUCTION

Count Lev Nikolayevich Tolstoy, also known as Leo Tolstoy (9 September 1828–20 November 1910), was a Russian writer, who primarily wrote novels and short stories. He was a master of realistic fiction. A believer in the power of love and non-violence, he gave up a life of wealth and pleasure in order to help the poor. Mohandas Karamchand Gandhi was a follower of Tolstoy's teachings and the two often wrote letters to each other.

Tolstoy's political thought is relevant in the twenty-first century as well. He expressed a deep discontent with the state, the church, the economy and the revolutionaries because of which he was recognized as a moral thinker and a social reformer.

- 'A Candle' is a powerful story that shows how God manifests his power and justice through goodness as opposed to evil.
- 'After the Dance' is a heart-wrenching story, that deals with the question whether one's life is determined by 'chance' or the environment one lives in?
- 'Albert' is about a man's struggle to find out what makes someone the best and the happiest.
- 'Alyosha the Pot' is a tragic story of love that does not culminate in a happy ending.
- 'An Old Acquaintance' is a riveting story of what transpires when a man comes face to face with an old acquaintance after many years.

- 'Does a Man Need Much Land?' is the story of Pahom, who thinks: 'if I had plenty of land, I shouldn't fear the Devil himself', a wish that is heeded by the Devil. However, in his greed for more land, Pahom stands to lose much more.
- 'A Spark Neglected Burns the House' is in the form of a parable, and talks about the virtue of forgiveness and reconciliation, and the harm that can befall people if the spark of revenge is not contained before it turns into fire.
- 'Lucerne' espouses the importance of kindness and compassion, and denounces the rich for their shallowness, self-absorption and insensitivity towards the unfortunate people around them.
- 'There are No Guilty People' is narrated from the point-of-view of an old beggar. The story questions the inequality and oppression faced by the underprivileged and the apathy of the rich and powerful towards them.
- 'God Sees the Truth, but Waits' is a heartwarming tale about the power of forgiveness. It is the story of Ivan Dmitrich Aksionov, who is wrongfully accused of a murder he didn't commit and spends twenty-six years in a prison in Siberia, where he eventually comes face-to-face with the real murderer.

1

A CANDLE

'Ye have heard that it hath been said, an eye for an eye and a tooth for a tooth: but I say unto you, That ye resist not evil.' ST. MATTHEW V. 38, 39.

It was in the time of serfdom—many years before Alexander II's liberation of the sixty million serfs in 1862. In those days the people were ruled by different kinds of lords. There were not a few who, remembering God, treated their slaves in a humane manner, and not as beasts of burden, while there were others who were seldom known to perform a kind or generous action; but the most barbarous and tyrannical of all were those former serfs who arose from the dirt and became princes.

It was this latter class who made life literally a burden to those who were unfortunate enough to come under their rule. Many of them had arisen from the ranks of the peasantry to become superintendents of noblemen's estates.

The peasants were obliged to work for their master a certain number of days each week. There was plenty of land and water and the soil was rich and fertile, while the meadows and forests were sufficient to supply the needs of both the peasants and their lord.

There was a certain nobleman who had chosen a superintendent from the peasantry on one of his other estates. No sooner had the power to govern been vested in this newly-made official than he began to practise the most outrageous cruelties upon the poor serfs who had been placed under his control. Although this man had a wife and two married daughters, and was making so much money that he could have lived happily without transgressing in any way against either God or man, yet he was filled with envy and jealousy and deeply sunk in sin.

Michael Simeonovitch began his persecutions by compelling the peasants to perform more days of service on the estate every week than the laws obliged them to work. He established a brickyard, in which he forced the men and women to do excessive labour, selling the bricks for his own profit.

On one occasion the overworked serfs sent a delegation to Moscow to complain of their treatment to their lord, but they obtained no satisfaction. When the poor peasants returned disconsolate from the nobleman their superintendent determined to have revenge for their boldness in going above him for redress, and their life and that of their fellow-victims became worse than before.

It happened that among the serfs there were some very treacherous people who would falsely accuse their fellows of wrong-doing and sow seeds of discord among the peasantry, whereupon Michael would become greatly enraged, while his poor subjects began to live in fear of their lives. When the superintendent passed through the village people would run and hide themselves as from a wild beast. Seeing thus the terror which he had struck to the hearts of the moujiks, Michael's treatment of them became still more vindictive, so that from over-work and ill-usage the lot of the poor serfs was indeed a hard one.

There was a time when it was possible for the peasants, when driven to despair, to devise means whereby they could rid themselves of an inhuman monster such as Simeonovitch, and so these unfortunate people began to consider whether something could not be done to relieve THEM of their intolerable yoke. They would hold little meetings in secret places to bewail their misery and to confer with one another as to which would be the best way to act. Now and then the boldest of the gathering would rise and address his companions in this strain: 'How much longer can we tolerate such a villain to rule over us? Let us make an end of it at once, for it were better for us to perish than to suffer. It is surely not a sin to kill such a devil in human form.'

It happened once, before the Easter holidays, that one of these meetings was held in the woods, where Michael had sent the serfs to make a clearance for their master. At noon they assembled to eat their dinner and to hold a consultation. 'Why can't we leave now?' said one. 'Very soon we shall be reduced to nothing. Already we are almost worked to death—there being no rest, night or day, either for us or our poor women. If anything should be done in a way not exactly to please him he will find fault and perhaps flog some of us to death—as was the case with poor Simeon, whom he killed not long ago. Only recently Anisim was tortured in irons till he died. We certainly cannot stand this much longer.'

'Yes,' said another, 'what is the use of waiting? Let us act at once. Michael will be here this evening, and will be certain to abuse us shamefully. Let us, then, thrust him from his horse and with one blow of an axe give him what he deserves, and thus end our misery. We can then dig a big hole and bury him like a dog, and no one will know what became of him. Now let us come to an agreement—to stand together as one man and not to betray one another.'

The last speaker was Vasili Minayeff, who, if possible, had more cause to complain of Michael's cruelty than any of his fellow-serfs. The superintendent was in the habit of flogging him severely every week, and he took also Vasili's wife to serve him as cook.

Accordingly, during the evening that followed this meeting in the woods Michael arrived on the scene on horseback. He began at once to find fault with the manner in which the work had been done, and to complain because some lime-trees had been cut down.

'I told you not to cut down any lime-trees!' shouted the enraged superintendent. 'Who did this thing? Tell me at once, or I shall flog every one of you!'

On investigation, a peasant named Sidor was pointed out as the guilty one, and his face was roundly slapped. Michael also severely punished Vasili, because he had not done sufficient work, after which the master rode safely home.

In the evening the serfs again assembled, and poor Vasili said: 'Oh, what kind of people ARE we, anyway? We are only sparrows, and not men at all! We agree to stand by each other, but as soon as the time for action comes we all run and hide. Once a lot of sparrows conspired against a hawk, but no sooner did the bird of prey appear than they sneaked off in the grass. Selecting one of the choicest sparrows, the hawk took it away to eat, after which the others came out crying, "Twee-twee!" and found that one was missing. "Who is killed?" they asked. "Vanka! Well, he deserved it." You, my friends, are acting in just the same manner. When Michael attacked Sidor you should have stood by your promise. Why didn't you arise, and with one stroke put an end to him and to our misery?'

The effect of this speech was to make the peasants more firm in their determination to kill their superintendent. The latter had already given orders that they should be ready to plough during the Easter holidays, and to sow the field with oats, whereupon the serfs became stricken with grief, and gathered in Vasili's house to hold another indignation meeting. 'If he has really forgotten God,' they said, 'and shall continue to commit such crimes against us, it is truly necessary that we should kill him. If not, let us perish, for it can make no difference to us now.'

This despairing programme, however, met with considerable opposition from a peaceably-inclined man named Peter Mikhayeff. 'Brethren,' said he, 'you are contemplating a grievous sin. The taking of human life is a very serious matter. Of course it is easy to end the mortal existence of a man, but what will become of the souls of those who commit the deed? If Michael continues to act toward us unjustly God will surely punish him. But, my friends, we must have patience.'

This pacific utterance only served to intensify the anger of Vasili. Said he: 'Peter is forever repeating the same old story, "It is a sin to kill anyone." Certainly it is sinful to murder; but we should consider the kind of man we are dealing with. We all know it is wrong to kill a good man, but even God would take away the life of such a dog as he is. It is our duty, if we have any love for mankind, to shoot a dog that is mad. It is a sin to let him live. If, therefore, we are to suffer at all, let it be in the interests of the people—and they will thank us for it. If we remain quiet any longer a flogging will be our only reward. You are talking nonsense, Mikhayeff. Why don't you think of the sin we shall be committing if we work during the Easter holidays—for you will refuse to work then yourself?'

'Well, then,' replied Peter, 'if they shall send me to plough, I will go. But I shall not be going of my own free will, and God will know whose sin it is, and shall punish the offender accordingly. Yet we must not forget him. Brethren, I am not giving you my own views only. The law of God is not to return evil for evil; indeed, if you try in this way to stamp out wickedness it will come upon you all the stronger. It is not difficult for you to kill the man, but his blood will surely stain your own soul. You may think you have killed a bad man—that you have gotten rid of evil—but you will soon find out that the seeds of still greater wickedness have been planted within you. If you yield to misfortune it will surely come to you.'

As Peter was not without sympathizers among the peasants, the poor serfs were consequently divided into two groups: the followers of Vasili and those who held the views of Mikhayeff.

On Easter Sunday no work was done. Toward the evening an elder came to the peasants from the nobleman's court and said: 'Our superintendent, Michael Simeonovitch, orders you to go tomorrow to plough the field for the oats.' Thus the official went through the village and directed the men to prepare for work the next day—some by the river and others by the roadway. The poor people were almost overcome with grief, many of them shedding tears, but none dared to disobey the orders of their master.

On the morning of Easter Monday, while the church bells were calling the inhabitants to religious services, and while every one else was about to enjoy a holiday, the unfortunate serfs started for the field to plough. Michael arose rather late and took a walk about the farm. The domestic servants were through with their work and had dressed themselves for the day, while Michael's wife and their widowed daughter (who was visiting them, as was her custom on holidays) had been to church and returned. A steaming samovar awaited them, and they began to drink tea with Michael, who, after lighting his pipe, called the elder to him.

'Well,' said the superintendent, 'have you ordered the moujiks to plough today?'

'Yes, sir, I did,' was the reply.

'Have they all gone to the field?'

'Yes, sir; all of them. I directed them myself where to begin.'

'That is all very well. You gave the orders, but are they ploughing? Go at once and see, and you may tell them that I shall be there after dinner. I shall expect to find one and a half acres done for every two ploughs, and the work must be well done; otherwise they shall be severely punished, notwithstanding the holiday.'

'I hear, sir, and obey.'

The elder started to go, but Michael called him back. After hesitating for some time, as if he felt very uneasy, he said: 'By the way, listen to what those scoundrels say about me. Doubtless some of them will curse me, and I want you to report the exact words. I know what villains they are. They don't find work at all pleasant. They would rather lie down all day and do nothing. They would like to eat and drink and make merry on holidays, but they forget that if the ploughing is not done it will soon be too late. So you go and listen to what is said, and tell it to me in detail. Go at once.'

'I hear, sir, and obey.'

Turning his back and mounting his horse, the elder was soon at the field where the serfs were hard at work.

It happened that Michael's wife, a very good-hearted woman, overheard the conversation which her husband had just been holding with the elder. Approaching him, she said: 'My good friend, Mishinka [diminutive of Michael], I beg of you to consider the importance and solemnity of this holy day. Do not sin, for Christ's sake. Let the poor moujiks go home.'

Michael laughed, but made no reply to his wife's humane request. Finally he said to her: 'You've not been whipped for a very long time, and now you have become bold enough to interfere in affairs that are not your own.'

'Mishinka,' she persisted, 'I have had a frightful dream concerning you. You had better let the moujiks go.'

'Yes,' said he; 'I perceive that you have gained so much flesh of late that you think you would not feel the whip. Lookout!'

Rudely thrusting his hot pipe against her cheek, Michael chased his wife from the room, after which he ordered his dinner. After eating a hearty meal consisting of cabbage-soup, roast pig, meat-cake, pastry with milk, jelly, sweet cakes, and vodka, he called his woman cook to him and ordered her to be seated and sing songs, Simeonovitch accompanying her on the guitar.

While the superintendent was thus enjoying himself to the

fullest satisfaction in the musical society of his cook the elder returned, and, making a low bow to his superior, proceeded to give the desired information concerning the serfs.

'Well,' asked Michael, 'did they plough?'

'Yes,' replied the elder; 'they have accomplished about half the field.'

'Is there no fault to be found?'

'Not that I could discover. The work seems to be well done. They are evidently afraid of you.'

'How is the soil?'

'Very good. It appears to be quite soft.'

'Well,' said Simeonovitch, after a pause, 'what did they say about me? Cursed me, I suppose?'

As the elder hesitated somewhat, Michael commanded him to speak and tell him the whole truth. 'Tell me all,' said he; 'I want to know their exact words. If you tell me the truth I shall reward you; but if you conceal anything from me you will be punished. See here, Catherine, pour out a glass of vodka to give him courage!'

After drinking to the health of his superior, the elder said to himself: 'It is not my fault if they do not praise him. I shall tell him the truth.' Then turning suddenly to the superintendent he said:

'They complain, Michael Simeonovitch! They complain bitterly.'

'But what did they say?' demanded Michael. 'Tell me!'

'Well, one thing they said was, "He does not believe in God."'

Michael laughed. 'Who said that?' he asked.

'It seemed to be their unanimous opinion. "He has been overcome by the Evil One," they said.'

'Very good,' laughed the superintendent; 'but tell me what each of them said. What did Vasili say?'

The elder did not wish to betray his people, but he had a certain grudge against Vasili, and he said: 'He cursed you more than did any of the others.'

'But what did he say?'

'It is awful to repeat it, sir. Vasili said, "He shall die like a dog, having no chance to repent!"'

'Oh, the villain!' exclaimed Michael. 'He would kill me if he were not afraid. All right, Vasili; we shall have an accounting with you. And Tishka—he called me a dog, I suppose?'

'Well,' said the elder, 'they all spoke of you in anything but complimentary terms; but it is mean of me to repeat what they said.'

'Mean or not you must tell me, I say!'

'Some of them declared that your back should be broken.'

Simeonovitch appeared to enjoy this immensely, for he laughed outright. 'We shall see whose back will be the first to be broken,' said he. 'Was that Tishka's opinion? While I did not suppose they would say anything good about me, I did not expect such curses and threats. And Peter Mikhayeff—was that fool cursing me too?'

'No; he did not curse you at all. He appeared to be the only silent one among them. Mikhayeff is a very wise moujik, and he surprises me very much. At his actions all the other peasants seemed amazed.'

'What did he do?'

'He did something remarkable. He was diligently ploughing, and as I approached him I heard some one singing very sweetly. Looking between the ploughshares, I observed a bright object shining.'

'Well, what was it? Hurry up!'

'It was a small, five-kopeck wax candle, burning brightly, and the wind was unable to blow it out. Peter, wearing a new shirt, sang beautiful hymns as he ploughed, and no matter how he handled the implement the candle continued to burn. In my presence he fixed the plough, shaking it violently, but the bright little object between the colters remained undisturbed.'

'And what did Mikhayeff say?'

'He said nothing—except when, on seeing me, he gave me the holy-day salutation, after which he went on his way singing and ploughing as before. I did not say anything to him, but, on approaching the other moujiks, I found that they were laughing and making sport of their silent companion. "It is a great sin to plough on Easter Monday," they said. "You could not get absolution from your sin if you were to pray all your life."'

'And did Mikhayeff make no reply?'

'He stood long enough to say: "There should be peace on earth and good-will to men," after which he resumed his ploughing and singing, the candle burning even more brightly than before.'

Simeonovitch had now ceased to ridicule, and, putting aside his guitar, his head dropped on his breast and he became lost in thought. Presently he ordered the elder and cook to depart, after which Michael went behind a screen and threw himself upon the bed. He was sighing and moaning, as if in great distress, when his wife came in and spoke kindly to him. He refused to listen to her, exclaiming:

'He has conquered me, and my end is near!'

'Mishinka,' said the woman, 'arise and go to the moujiks in the field. Let them go home, and everything will be all right. Heretofore you have run far greater risks without any fear, but now you appear to be very much alarmed.'

'He has conquered me!' he repeated. 'I am lost!'

'What do you mean?' demanded his wife, angrily. 'If you will go and do as I tell you there will be no danger. Come, Mishinka,' she added, tenderly; 'I shall have the saddle-horse brought for you at once.'

When the horse arrived the woman persuaded her husband to mount the animal, and to fulfil her request concerning the serfs. When he reached the village a woman opened the gate for him to enter, and as he did so the inhabitants, seeing the brutal superintendent whom everybody feared, ran to hide themselves in their houses, gardens, and other secluded places.

At length Michael reached the other gate, which he found closed also, and, being unable to open it himself while seated on his horse, he called loudly for assistance. As no one responded to his shouts he dismounted and opened the gate, but as he was about to remount, and had one foot in the stirrup, the horse became frightened at some pigs and sprang suddenly to one side. The superintendent fell across the fence and a very sharp picket pierced his stomach, when Michael fell unconscious to the ground.

Toward the evening, when the serfs arrived at the village gate, their horses refused to enter. On looking around, the peasants discovered the dead body of their superintendent lying face downward in a pool of blood, where he had fallen from the fence. Peter Mikhayeff alone had sufficient courage to dismount and approach the prostrate form, his companions riding around the village and entering by way of the back yards. Peter closed the dead man's eyes, after which he put the body in a wagon and took it home.

When the nobleman learned of the fatal accident which had befallen his superintendent, and of the brutal treatment which he had meted out to those under him, he freed the serfs, exacting a small rent for the use of his land and the other agricultural opportunities.

And thus the peasants clearly understood that the power of God is manifested not in evil, but in goodness.

2

AFTER THE DANCE

'AND you say that a man cannot, of himself, understand what is good and evil; that it is all environment, that the environment swamps the man. But I believe it is all chance. Take my own case...'

Thus spoke our excellent friend, Ivan Vasilievich, after a conversation between us on the impossibility of improving individual character without a change of the conditions under which men live. Nobody had actually said that one could not of oneself understand good and evil; but it was a habit of Ivan Vasilievich to answer in this way the thoughts aroused in his own mind by conversation, and to illustrate those thoughts by relating incidents in his own life. He often quite forgot the reason for his story in telling it; but he always told it with great sincerity and feeling.

He did so now.

'Take my own case. My whole life was moulded, not by environment, but by something quite different.'

'By what, then?' we asked.

'Oh, that is a long story. I should have to tell you about a great many things to make you understand.'

'Well, tell us then.'

Ivan Vasilievich thought a little, and shook his head.

'My whole life,' he said, 'was changed in one night, or, rather, morning.'

'Why, what happened?' one of us asked.

'What happened was that I was very much in love. I have been in love many times, but this was the most serious of all. It is a thing of the past; she has married daughters now. It was Varinka B——.' Ivan Vasilievich mentioned her surname. 'Even at fifty she is remarkably handsome; but in her youth, at eighteen, she was exquisite—tall, slender, graceful, and stately. Yes, stately is the word; she held herself very erect, by instinct as it were; and carried her head high, and that together with her beauty and height gave her a queenly air in spite of being thin, even bony one might say. It might indeed have been deterring had it not been for her smile, which was always gay and cordial, and for the charming light in her eyes and for her youthful sweetness.'

'What an entrancing description you give, Ivan Vasilievich!'

'Description, indeed! I could not possibly describe her so that you could appreciate her. But that does not matter; what I am going to tell you happened in the forties. I was at that time a student in a provincial university. I don't know whether it was a good thing or no, but we had no political clubs, no theories in our universities then. We were simply young and spent our time as young men do, studying and amusing ourselves. I was a very gay, lively, careless fellow, and had plenty of money too. I had a fine horse, and used to go tobogganing with the young ladies. Skating had not yet come into fashion. I went to drinking parties with my comrades—in those days we drank nothing but champagne—if we had no champagne we drank nothing at all. We never drank vodka, as they do now. Evening parties and balls were my favourite amusements. I danced well, and was not an ugly fellow.'

'Come, there is no need to be modest,' interrupted a lady near him. 'We have seen your photograph. Not ugly, indeed! You were a handsome fellow.'

'Handsome, if you like. That does not matter. When my love for her was at its strongest, on the last day of the carnival, I was at a ball at the provincial marshal's, a good-natured old man, rich and hospitable, and a court chamberlain. The guests were welcomed by his wife, who was as good-natured as himself. She was dressed in puce-coloured velvet, and had a diamond diadem on her forehead, and her plump, old white shoulders and bosom were bare like the portraits of Empress Elizabeth, the daughter of Peter the Great.

'It was a delightful ball. It was a splendid room, with a gallery for the orchestra, which was famous at the time, and consisted of serfs belonging to a musical landowner. The refreshments were magnificent, and the champagne flowed in rivers. Though I was fond of champagne I did not drink that night, because without it I was drunk with love. But I made up for it by dancing waltzes and polkas till I was ready to drop—of course, whenever possible, with Varinka. She wore a white dress with a pink sash, white shoes, and white kid gloves, which did not quite reach to her thin pointed elbows. A disgusting engineer named Anisimov robbed me of the mazurka with her—to this day I cannot forgive him. He asked her for the dance the minute she arrived, while I had driven to the hairdresser's to get a pair of gloves, and was late. So I did not dance the mazurka with her, but with a German girl to whom I had previously paid a little attention; but I am afraid I did not behave very politely to her that evening. I hardly spoke or looked at her, and saw nothing but the tall, slender figure in a white dress, with a pink sash, a flushed, beaming, dimpled face, and sweet, kind eyes. I was not alone; they were all looking at her with admiration, the men and women alike, although she outshone all of them. They could not help admiring her.

'Although I was not nominally her partner for the mazurka, I did as a matter of fact dance nearly the whole time with her. She always came forward boldly the whole length of the room to pick me out. I flew to meet her without waiting to be chosen, and she thanked me with a smile for my intuition. When I was brought up to her with somebody else, and she guessed wrongly, she took the other man's hand with a shrug of her slim shoulders, and smiled at me regretfully.

'Whenever there was a waltz figure in the mazurka, I waltzed with her for a long time, and breathing fast and smiling, she would say, "Encore"; and I went on waltzing and waltzing, as though unconscious of any bodily existence.'

'Come now, how could you be unconscious of it with your arm round her waist? You must have been conscious, not only of your own existence, but of hers,' said one of the party.

Ivan Vasilievich cried out, almost shouting in anger: 'There you are, moderns all over! Nowadays you think of nothing but the body. It was different in our day. The more I was in love the less corporeal was she in my eyes. Nowadays you think of nothing but the body. It was different in our day. The more I was in love the less corporeal was she in my eyes. Nowadays you set legs, ankles, and I don't know what. You undress the women you are in love with. In my eyes, as Alphonse Karr said—and he was a good writer—"the one I loved was always draped in robes of bronze." We never thought of doing so; we tried to veil her nakedness, like Noah's good-natured son. Oh, well, you can't understand.'

'Don't pay any attention to him. Go on,' said one of them.

'Well, I danced for the most part with her, and did not notice how time was passing. The musicians kept playing the same mazurka tunes over and over again in desperate exhaustion—you know what it is towards the end of a ball. Papas and mammas were already getting up from the card-tables in the drawing-room in expectation of supper, the men-servants were running to and fro bringing in things. It was nearly three o'clock. I had to make the most of the last minutes. I chose her again for the mazurka, and for the hundredth time we danced across the room.

'"The quadrille after supper is mine," I said, taking her to her place.

'"Of course, if I am not carried off home," she said, with a smile.

'"I won't give you up," I said.

'"Give me my fan, anyhow," she answered.

'"I am so sorry to part with it," I said, handing her a cheap white fan.

'"Well, here's something to console you," she said, plucking a feather out of the fan, and giving it to me.

'I took the feather, and could only express my rapture and gratitude with my eyes. I was not only pleased and gay, I was happy, delighted; I was good, I was not myself but some being not of this earth, knowing nothing of evil. I hid the feather in my glove, and stood there unable to tear myself away from her.

'"Look, they are urging father to dance," she said to me, pointing to the tall, stately figure of her father, a colonel with silver epaulettes, who was standing in the doorway with some ladies.

'"Varinka, come here!" exclaimed our hostess, the lady with the diamond ferronniere and with shoulders like Elizabeth, in a loud voice.

'Varinka went to the door, and I followed her.

'"Persuade your father to dance the mazurka with you, ma chere. Do, please, Peter Valdislavovich," she said, turning to the colonel.

'Varinka's father was a very handsome, well-preserved old man. He had a good colour, moustaches curled in the style of Nicolas I., and white whiskers which met the moustaches. His hair was combed on to his forehead, and a bright smile, like his daughter's, was on his lips and in his eyes. He was splendidly set up, with a broad military chest, on which he wore some decorations, and he had powerful shoulders and long slim legs. He was that ultra-military type produced by the discipline of Emperor Nicolas I.

'When we approached the door the colonel was just refusing to dance, saying that he had quite forgotten how; but at that instant he smiled, swung his arm gracefully around to the left, drew his sword from its sheath, handed it to an obliging young man who stood near, and smoothed his suede glove on his right hand.

'"Everything must be done according to rule," he said with a smile. He took the hand of his daughter, and stood one-quarter turned, waiting for the music.

'At the first sound of the mazurka, he stamped one foot smartly, threw the other forward, and, at first slowly and smoothly, then buoyantly and impetuously, with stamping of feet and clicking of boots, his tall, imposing figure moved the length of the room. Varinka swayed gracefully beside him, rhythmically and easily, making her steps short or long, with her little feet in their white satin slippers.

'All the people in the room followed every movement of the couple. As for me I not only admired, I regarded them with enraptured sympathy. I was particularly impressed with the old gentleman's boots. They were not the modern pointed affairs, but were made of cheap leather, squared-toed, and evidently built by the regimental cobbler. In order that his daughter might dress and go out in society, he did not buy fashionable boots, but wore home-made ones, I thought, and his square toes seemed to me most touching. It was obvious that in his time he had been a good dancer; but now he was too heavy, and his legs had not spring enough for all the beautiful steps he tried to take. Still, he contrived to go twice round the room. When at the end, standing with legs apart, he suddenly clicked his feet together and fell on one knee, a bit heavily, and she danced gracefully around him, smiling and adjusting her skirt, the whole room applauded.

'Rising with an effort, he tenderly took his daughter's face between his hands. He kissed her on the forehead, and brought her to me, under the impression that I was her partner for the mazurka. I said I was not. "Well, never mind. just go around the room once with her," he said, smiling kindly, as he replaced his sword in the sheath.

'As the contents of a bottle flow readily when the first drop has been poured, so my love for Varinka seemed to set free the whole force of loving within me. In surrounding her it embraced the world. I loved the hostess with her diadem and her shoulders like Elizabeth, and her husband and her guests and her footmen, and even the engineer Anisimov who felt peevish towards me. As for Varinka's father, with his home-made boots and his kind smile, so like her own, I felt a sort of tenderness for him that was almost rapture.

'After supper I danced the promised quadrille with her, and though I had been infinitely happy before, I grew still happier every moment.

'We did not speak of love. I neither asked myself nor her whether she loved me. It was quite enough to know that I loved her. And I had only one fear—that something might come to interfere with my great joy.

'When I went home, and began to undress for the night, I found it quite out of the question. held the little feather out of her fan in my hand, and one of her gloves which she gave me when I helped her into the carriage after her mother. Looking at these things, and without closing my eyes I could see her before me as she was for an instant when she had to choose between two partners. She tried to guess what kind of person was represented in me, and I could hear her sweet voice as she said, "Pride—am I right?" and merrily gave me her hand. At supper she took the first sip from my glass of champagne, looking at me over the rim with her caressing glance. But, plainest of all, I could see her as she danced with her father, gliding along beside him, and looking at the admiring observers with pride and happiness.

'He and she were united in my mind in one rush of pathetic

tenderness.

'I was living then with my brother, who has since died. He disliked going out, and never went to dances; and besides, he was busy preparing for his last university examinations, and was leading a very regular life. He was asleep. I looked at him, his head buried in the pillow and half covered with the quilt; and I affectionately pitied him, pitied him for his ignorance of the bliss I was experiencing. Our serf Petrusha had met me with a candle, ready to undress me, but I sent him away. His sleepy face and tousled hair seemed to me so touching. Trying not to make a noise, I went to my room on tiptoe and sat down on my bed. No, I was too happy; I could not sleep. Besides, it was too hot in the rooms. Without taking off my uniform, I went quietly into the hall, put on my overcoat, opened the front door and stepped out into the street.

'It was after four when I had left the ball; going home and stopping there a while had occupied two hours, so by the time I went out it was dawn. It was regular carnival weather—foggy, and the road full of water-soaked snow just melting, and water dripping from the eaves. Varinka's family lived on the edge of town near a large field, one end of which was a parade ground: at the other end was a boarding-school for young ladies. I passed through our empty little street and came to the main thoroughfare, where I met pedestrians and sledges laden with wood, the runners grating the road. The horses swung with regular paces beneath their shining yokes, their backs covered with straw mats and their heads wet with rain; while the drivers, in enormous boots, splashed through the mud beside the sledges. All this, the very horses themselves, seemed to me stimulating and fascinating, full of suggestion.

'When I approached the field near their house, I saw at one end of it, in the direction of the parade ground, something very huge and black, and I heard sounds of fife and drum proceeding from it. My heart had been full of song, and I had heard in imagination the tune of the mazurka, but this was very harsh music. It was not pleasant.

'"What can that be?" I thought, and went towards the sound by a slippery path through the centre of the field. Walking about a hundred paces, I began to distinguish many black objects through the mist. They were evidently soldiers. "It is probably a drill," I thought.

'So I went along in that direction in company with a blacksmith, who wore a dirty coat and an apron, and was carrying something. He walked ahead of me as we approached the place. The soldiers in black uniforms stood in two rows, facing each other motionless, their guns at rest. Behind them stood the fifes and drums, incessantly repeating the same unpleasant tune.

'"What are they doing?" I asked the blacksmith, who halted at my side.

'"A Tartar is being beaten through the ranks for his attempt to desert," said the blacksmith in an angry tone, as he looked intently at the far end of the line.

'I looked in the same direction, and saw between the files something horrid approaching me. The thing that approached was a man, stripped to the waist, fastened with cords to the guns of two soldiers who were leading him. At his side an officer in overcoat and cap was walking, whose figure had a familiar look. The victim advanced under the blows that rained upon him from both sides, his whole body plunging, his feet dragging through the snow. Now he threw himself backward, and the subalterns who led him thrust him forward. Now he fell forward, and they pulled him up short; while ever at his side marched the tall officer, with firm and nervous pace. It was Varinka's father, with his rosy face and white moustache.

'At each stroke the man, as if amazed, turned his face, grimacing with pain, towards the side whence the blow came, and showing his white teeth repeated the same words over and over.

But I could only hear what the words were when he came quite near. He did not speak them, he sobbed them out—"'Brothers, have mercy on me! Brothers, have mercy on me!" But the brothers had, no mercy, and when the procession came close to me, I saw how a soldier who stood opposite me took a firm step forward and lifting his stick with a whirr, brought it down upon the man's back. The man plunged forward, but the subalterns pulled him back, and another blow came down from the other side, then from this side and then from the other. The colonel marched beside him, and looking now at his feet and now at the man, inhaled the air, puffed out his cheeks, and breathed it out between his protruded lips. When they passed the place where I stood, I caught a glimpse between the two files of the back of the man that was being punished. It was something so many-coloured, wet, red, unnatural, that I could hardly believe it was a human body.

'"My God!" muttered the blacksmith.

'The procession moved farther away. The blows continued to rain upon the writhing, falling creature; the fifes shrilled and the drums beat, and the tall imposing figure of the colonel moved alongside the man, just as before. Then, suddenly, the colonel stopped, and rapidly approached a man in the ranks.

'"I'll teach you to hit him gently," I heard his furious voice say. "Will you pat him like that? Will you?" and I saw how his strong hand in the suede glove struck the weak, bloodless, terrified soldier for not bringing down his stick with sufficient strength on the red neck of the Tartar.

'"Bring new sticks!" he cried, and looking round, he saw me. Assuming an air of not knowing me, and with a ferocious, angry frown, he hastily turned away. I felt so utterly ashamed that I didn't know where to look. It was as if I had been detected in a disgraceful act. I dropped my eyes, and quickly hurried home. All the way I had the drums beating and the fifes whistling in my ears. And I heard the words, "Brothers, have mercy on me!" or "Will you pat him? Will you?" My heart was full of physical disgust that was almost sickness. So much so that I halted several times on my way, for I had the feeling that I was going to be really sick from all the horrors that possessed me at that sight. I do not remember how I got home and got to bed. But the moment I was about to fall asleep I heard and saw again all that had happened, and I sprang up.

'"Evidently he knows something I do not know," I thought about the colonel. "If I knew what he knows I should certainly grasp—understand—what I have just seen, and it would not cause me such suffering."

'But however much I thought about it, I could not understand the thing that the colonel knew. It was evening before I could get to sleep, and then only after calling on a friend and drinking till I was quite drunk.

'Do you think I had come to the conclusion that the deed I had witnessed was wicked? Oh, no. Since it was done with such assurance, and was recognized by every one as indispensable, they doubtless knew something which I did not know. So I thought, and tried to understand. But no matter, I could never understand it, then or afterwards. And not being able to grasp it, I could not enter the service as I had intended. I don't mean only the military service: I did not enter the Civil Service either. And so I have been of no use whatever, as you can see.

'"Yes, we know how useless you've been," said one of us. 'Tell us, rather, how many people would be of any use at all if it hadn't been for you.'

'"Oh, that's utter nonsense," said Ivan Vasilievich, with genuine annoyance.

'"Well; and what about the love affair?"

'My love? It decreased from that day. When, as often happened, she looked dreamy and meditative, I instantly recollected the colonel on the parade ground, and I felt so awkward and uncomfortable that I began to see her less frequently. So my love came to naught. Yes; such chances arise, and they alter and direct a man's whole life,' he said in summing up. 'And you say…'

3

ALBERT

It was indeed cold outside, but Albert, heated by the liquor he had drunk and by the dispute, did not feel it. On reaching the street he looked round and rubbed his hands joyfully.

The street was empty, but the long row of lamps still burned with ruddy light; the sky was clear and starry. 'There now!' he said, addressing the lighted window of Delesov's lodging, thrusting his hands into his trouser pockets under his cape, and stooping forward. He went with heavy, uncertain steps down the street to the right. He felt an unusual weight in his legs and stomach, something made a noise in his head, and some invisible force was throwing him from side to side, but he still went on in the direction of Anna Ivanovna's house.

Strange, incoherent thoughts passed through his mind. Now he remembered his last altercation with Zakhar, then for some reason the sea and his first arrival in Russia by steamboat, then a happy night he had passed with a friend in a small shop he was passing, then suddenly a familiar motif began singing itself in his imagination, and he remembered the object of his passion and the dreadful night in the theatre.

Despite their incoherence all these memories presented themselves so clearly to his mind that, closing his eyes, he did not know which was the more real: what he was doing, or what he was thinking. He did not realize or feel how his legs were moving, how he swayed and bumped against the wall, how he looked around him, or passed from street to street. He realized and felt only the things that, intermingling and fantastically following one another, rose in his imagination.

Passing along the Little Morskaya Street, Albert stumbled and fell. Coming to his senses for a moment he saw an immense and splendid building before him and went on. In the sky no stars, nor moon, nor dawn, were visible, nor were there any street lamps, but everything was clearly outlined. In the windows of the building that towered at the end of the street lights were shining, but those lights quivered like reflections. The building stood out nearer and nearer and clearer and clearer before him. But the lights disappeared directly he entered the wide portals. All was dark within. Solitary footsteps resounded under the vaulted ceiling, and some shadows slit rapidly away as he approached.

'Why have I come here?' thought he; but some irresistible force drew him on into the depths of the immense hall. There was some kind of platform, around which some small people stood silently.

'Who is going to speak?' asked Albert. No one replied, except that someone pointed to the platform. A tall thin man with bristly hair and wearing a particoloured dressing-gown was already standing there, and Albert immediately recognized his friend Petrov.

'How strange that he should be here!' thought he.

'No, brothers!' Petrov was saying, pointing to someone. 'You did not understand a man living among you; you have not understood him! He is not a mercenary artist, not a mechanical performer, not a lunatic or a lost man. He is a genius—a great musical genius who has perished among you unnoticed and unappreciated!'

Albert at once understood of whom his friend was speaking,

but not wishing to embarrass him he modestly lowered his head.

'The holy fire that we all serve has consumed him like a blade of straw!' the voice went on, 'but he has fulfilled all that God implanted in him and should therefore be called a great man. You could despise, torment, humiliate him,' the voice continued, growing louder and louder—'but he was, is, and will be, immeasurably higher than you all. He is happy, he is kind. He loves or despises all alike, but serves only that which was implanted in him from above. He loves but one thing—beauty, the one indubitable blessing in the world. Yes, such is the man! Fall prostrate before him, all of you! On your knees!' he cried aloud.

But another voice came mildly from the opposite corner of the hall: 'I do not wish to bow my knees before him,' said the voice, which Albert immediately recognized as Delesov's. 'Wherein is he great? Why should we bow before him? Did he behave honourably and justly? Has he been of any use to society? Don't we know how he borrowed money and did not return it, and how he carried away his fellow-artist's violin and pawned it?...'

('Oh God, how does he know all that?' thought Albert, hanging his head still lower.)

'Do we not know how he flattered the most insignificant people, flattered them for the sake of money?' Delesov continued —'Don't we know how he was expelled from the theatre? And how Anna Ivanovna wanted to send him to the police?'

('O God! That is all true, but defend me, Thou who alone knowest why I did it!' muttered Albert.)

'Cease, for shame!' Petrov's voice began again. 'What right have you to accuse him? Have you lived his life? Have you experienced his rapture? ('True, true!' whispered Albert.)

'Art is the highest manifestation of power in man. It is given to a few of the elect, and raises the chosen one to such a height as turns the head and makes it difficult for him to remain sane. In Art, as in every struggle, there are heroes who have devoted themselves entirely to its service and have perished without having reached the goal.'

Petrov stopped, and Albert raised his head and cried out: 'True, true!' but his voice died away without a sound.

'It does not concern you,' said the artist Petrov, turning to him severely. 'Yes, humiliate and despise him,' he continued, 'but yet he is the best and happiest of you all.'

Albert, who had listened to these words with rapture in his soul, could not restrain himself, and went up to his friend wishing to kiss him.

'Go away! I do not know you!' Petrov said, 'Go your way, or you won't get there.'

'Just see how the drink's got hold of you! You won't get there,' shouted a policeman at the crossroad.

Albert stopped, collected his strength and, trying not to stagger, turned into the side street.

Only a few more steps were left to Anna Ivanovna's door. From the hall of her house the light fell on the snow in the courtyard, and sledges and carriages stood at the gate.

Holding onto the banister with his numbed hands, he ran up the steps and rang. The sleepy face of a maid appeared in the opening of the doorway, and she looked angrily at Albert.

'You can't!' she cried. 'The orders are not to let you in,' and she slammed the door.

The sound of music and of women's voices reached the steps. Albert sat down, leaned his head against the wall, and closed his eyes. Immediately a throng of disconnected but kindred visions beset him with renewed force, engulfed him in their waves, and bore him away into the free and beautiful realm of dreams.

'Yes, he was the best and happiest!' ran involuntarily through his imagination.

The sounds of a polka came through the door. These sounds also told him that he was the best and happiest. The bells in the nearest church rang out for early service, and these bells also said:

'Yes, he is the best and happiest!'...

'I will go back to the hall,' thought Albert. 'Petrov must tell me much more.'

But there was no one in the hall now, and instead of the artist Petrov, Albert himself stood on the platform and played on the violin all that the voice had said before. But the violin was of strange construction; it was made of glass and it had to be held in both hands and slowly pressed to the breast to make it produce sounds. The sounds were the most delicate and delightful Albert had ever heard. The closer he pressed the violin to his breast the more joyful and tender he felt. The louder the sounds grew the faster the shadows dispersed and the brighter the walls of the hall were lit up by transparent light. But it was necessary to play the violin very warily so as not to break it. He played the glass instrument very carefully and well. He played such things as he felt no one would ever hear again.

He was beginning to grow tired when another distant, muffled sound distracted his attention. It was the sound of a bell, but it spoke words:

'Yes,' said the bell, droning somewhere high up and far away, 'he seems to you pitiful, you despise him, yet he is the best and happiest of men! No one will ever again play that instrument.'

These familiar words suddenly seemed so wise, so new, and so true to Albert that he stopped playing and, trying not to move, raised his arms and eyes to heaven. He felt that he was beautiful and happy. Although there was no one else in the hall he expanded his chest and stood on the platform with head proudly erect so that all might see him.

Suddenly someone's hand lightly touched his shoulder; he turned and saw a woman in the faint light. She looked at him sadly and shook her head deprecatingly. He immediately realized that what he was doing was bad, and felt ashamed of himself.

'Whither?' he asked her.

She again gave him a long fixed look and sadly inclined her head. It was she—none other than she whom he loved, and her garments were the same; on her full white neck a string of pearls, and her superb arms bare to above the elbow. She took his hand and led him out of the hall.

'The exit is on the other side,' said Albert, but without replying she smiled and led him out.

At the threshold of the hall Albert saw the moon and some water. But the water was not below as it usually is, nor was the moon a white circle in one place up above as it usually is. Moon and water were together and everywhere—above, below, at the sides, and all around them both. Albert threw himself with her into the moon and the water, and realized that he could now embrace her, whom he loved more than anything in the world. He embraced her and felt unutterable happiness.

'Is this not a dream?' he asked himself. But no! It was more than reality: it was reality and recollection combined. Then he felt that the unutterable bliss he had at that moment enjoyed had passed and would never return.

'What am I weeping for?' he asked her.

She looked at him silently and sadly. Albert understood what she meant by that.

'But how can it be, since I am alive?' he muttered.

Without replying or moving she looked straight before her.

'This is terrible! How can I explain to her that I am alive?' he thought with horror. 'O Lord! I am alive, do understand me!' he whispered.

'He is the best and happiest!' a voice was saying.

But something was pressing more and more heavily on Albert. Whether it was the moon and the water, her embraces, or his tears, he did not know, but he felt he would not be able to say all that was necessary, and that soon all would be over.

Two visitors, leaving Anna Ivanovna's house, stumbled over Albert, who lay stretched out on the threshold. One of them went back and called the hostess.

'Why, this is inhuman!' he said. 'You might let a man freeze like that!'

'Ah, that is Albert! I'm sick to death of him!' replied the hostess.

'Annushka, lay him down somewhere in a room,' she said to the maid.

'But I am alive—why bury me?' muttered Albert, as they carried him insensible into the room.

4

ALYOSHA THE POT

Alyosha was the younger brother. He was called the Pot, because his mother had once sent him with a pot of milk to the deacon's wife, and he had stumbled against something and broken it. His mother had beaten him, and the children had teased him. Since then he was nicknamed the Pot.

Alyosha was a tiny, thin little fellow, with ears like wings, and a huge nose. 'Alyosha has a nose that looks like a dog on a hill!' the children used to call after him. Alyosha went to the village school, but was not good at lessons; besides, there was so little time to learn. His elder brother was in town, working for a merchant, so Alyosha had to help his father from a very early age. When he was no more than six he used to go out with the girls to watch the cows and sheep in the pasture, and a little later he looked after the horses by day and by night. And at twelve years of age he had already begun to plough and to drive the cart. The skill was there though the strength was not. He was always cheerful. Whenever the children made fun of him, he would either laugh or be silent. When his father scolded him he would stand mute and listen attentively, and as soon as the scolding was over would smile and go on with his work. Alyosha was nineteen when his brother was taken as a soldier. So his father placed him with the merchant as a yard-porter.

He was given his brother's old boots, his father's old coat and cap, and was taken to town. Alyosha was delighted with his clothes, but the merchant was not impressed by his appearance.

'I thought you would bring me a man in Simeon's place,' he said, scanning Alyosha; 'and you've brought me THIS! What's the good of him?'

'He can do everything; look after horses and drive. He's a good one to work. He looks rather thin, but he's tough enough. And he's very willing.'

'He looks it. All right; we'll see what we can do with him.'

So Alyosha remained at the merchant's.

The family was not a large one. It consisted of the merchant's wife: her old mother: a married son poorly educated who was in his father's business: another son, a learned one who had finished school and entered the university, but having been expelled, was living at home: and a daughter who still went to school.

They did not take to Alyosha at first. He was uncouth, badly dressed, and had no manner, but they soon got used to him. Alyosha worked even better than his brother had done; he was really very willing. They sent him on all sorts of errands, but he did everything quickly and readily, going from one task to another without stopping. And so here, just as at home, all the work was put upon his shoulders. The more he did, the more he was given to do. His mistress, her old mother, the son, the daughter, the clerk, and the cook—all ordered him about, and sent him from one place to another.

'Alyosha, do this! Alyosha, do that! What! have you forgotten, Alyosha? Mind you, don't forget, Alyosha!' was heard from morning till night. And Alyosha ran here, looked after this and that, forgot nothing, found time for everything, and was always cheerful.

His brother's old boots were soon worn out, and his master scolded him for going about in tatters with his toes sticking out. He ordered another pair to be bought for him in the market.

Alyosha was delighted with his new boots, but was angry with his feet when they ached at the end of the day after so much running about. And then he was afraid that his father would be annoyed when he came to town for his wages, to find that his master had deducted the cost of the boots. In the winter Alyosha used to get up before daybreak. He would chop the wood, sweep the yard, feed the cows and horses, light the stoves, clean the boots, prepare the samovars and polish them afterwards; or the clerk would get him to bring up the goods; or the cook would set him to knead the bread and clean the saucepans. Then he was sent to town on various errands, to bring the daughter home from school, or to get some olive oil for the old mother. 'Why the devil have you been so long?' first one, then another, would say to him. Why should they go? Alyosha can go.

'Alyosha! Alyosha!' And Alyosha ran here and there. He breakfasted in snatches while he was working, and rarely managed to get his dinner at the proper hour. The cook used to scold him for being late, but she was sorry for him all the same, and would keep something hot for his dinner and supper. At holiday times there was more work than ever, but Alyosha liked holidays because everybody gave him a tip. Not much certainly, but it would amount up to about sixty kopeks [1s 2d] his very own money. For Alyosha never set eyes on his wages. His father used to come and take them from the merchant, and only scold Alyosha for wearing out his boots.

When he had saved up two roubles [4s], by the advice of the cook he bought himself a red knitted jacket, and was so happy when he put it on, that he couldn't close his mouth for joy. Alyosha was not talkative; when he spoke at all, he spoke abruptly, with his head turned away.

When told to do anything, or asked if he could do it, he would say yes without the smallest hesitation, and set to work at once.

Alyosha did not know any prayer; and had forgotten what

his mother had taught him. But he prayed just the same, every morning and every evening, prayed with his hands, crossing himself.

He lived like this for about a year and a half, and towards the end of the second year a most startling thing happened to him. He discovered one day, to his great surprise, that, in addition to the relation of usefulness existing between people, there was also another, a peculiar relation of quite a different character. Instead of a man being wanted to clean boots, and go on errands and harness horses, he is not wanted to be of any service at all, but another human being wants to serve him and pet him. Suddenly Alyosha felt he was such a man.

He made this discovery through the cook Ustinia. She was young, had no parents, and worked as hard as Alyosha. He felt for the first time in his life that he—not his services, but he himself— was necessary to another human being. When his mother used to be sorry for him, he had taken no notice of her. It had seemed to him quite natural, as though he were feeling sorry for himself. But here was Ustinia, a perfect stranger, and sorry for him. She would save him some hot porridge, and sit watching him, her chin propped on her bare arm, with the sleeve rolled up, while he was eating it. When he looked at her she would begin to laugh, and he would laugh too.

This was such a new, strange thing to him that it frightened Alyosha.

He feared that it might interfere with his work. But he was pleased, nevertheless, and when he glanced at the trousers that Ustinia had mended for him, he would shake his head and smile. He would often think of her while at work, or when running on errands. 'A fine girl, Ustinia!' he sometimes exclaimed.

Ustinia used to help him whenever she could, and he helped her. She told him all about her life; how she had lost her parents; how her aunt had taken her in and found a place for her in the town; how the merchant's son had tried to take liberties with her, and how she had rebuffed him. She liked to talk, and Alyosha liked to listen to her. He had heard that peasants who came up to work in the towns frequently got married to servant girls. On one occasion she asked him if his parents intended marrying him soon. He said that he did not know; that he did not want to marry any of the village girls.

'Have you taken a fancy to someone, then?'

'I would marry you, if you'd be willing.'

'Get along with you, Alyosha the Pot; but you've found your tongue, haven't you?' she exclaimed, slapping him on the back with a towel she held in her hand. 'Why shouldn't I?' At Shrovetide Alyosha's father came to town for his wages. It had come to the ears of the merchant's wife that Alyosha wanted to marry Ustinia, and she disapproved of it. 'What will be the use of her with a baby?' she thought, and informed her husband.

The merchant gave the old man Alyosha's wages.

'How is my lad getting on?' he asked. 'I told you he was willing.'

'That's all right, as far as it goes, but he's taken some sort of nonsense into his head. He wants to marry our cook. Now I don't approve of married servants. We won't have them in the house.'

'Well, now, who would have thought the fool would think of such a thing?' the old man exclaimed. 'But don't you worry. I'll soon settle that.' He went into the kitchen, and sat down at the table waiting for his son.

Alyosha was out on an errand, and came back breathless.

'I thought you had some sense in you; but what's this you've taken into your head?' his father began.

'I? Nothing.'

'How, nothing? They tell me you want to get married. You shall get married when the time comes. I'll find you a decent wife, not some town hussy.'

His father talked and talked, while Alyosha stood still and sighed. When his father had quite finished, Alyosha smiled.

'All right. I'll drop it.'

'Now that's what I call sense.'

When he was left alone with Ustinia he told her what his father had said. (She had listened at the door.)

'It's no good; it can't come off. Did you hear? He was angry—won't have it at any price.'

Ustinia cried into her apron.

Alyosha shook his head.

'What's to be done? We must do as we're told.'

'Well, are you going to give up that nonsense, as your father told you?' his mistress asked, as he was putting up the shutters in the evening. 'To be sure we are,' Alyosha replied with a smile, and then burst into tears.

From that day Alyosha went about his work as usual, and no longer talked to Ustinia about their getting married. One day in Lent the clerk told him to clear the snow from the roof. Alyosha climbed on to the roof and swept away all the snow; and, while he was still raking out some frozen lumps from the gutter, his foot slipped and he fell over. Unfortunately he did not fall on the snow, but on a piece of iron over the door.

Ustinia came running up, together with the merchant's daughter.

'Have you hurt yourself, Alyosha?'

'Ah! no, it's nothing.'

But he could not raise himself when he tried to, and began to smile.

He was taken into the lodge. The doctor arrived, examined him, and asked where he felt the pain.

'I feel it all over,' he said. 'But it doesn't matter. I'm only afraid master will be annoyed. Father ought to be told.' Alyosha lay in bed for two days, and on the third day they sent for the priest.

'Are you really going to die?' Ustinia asked.

'Of course I am. You can't go on living for ever. You must go when the time comes.' Alyosha spoke rapidly as usual. 'Thank you, Ustinia. You've been very good to me. What a lucky thing they didn't let us marry! Where should we have been now? It's much better as it is.'

When the priest came, he prayed with his bands and with his heart. 'As it is good here when you obey and do no harm to others, so it will be there,' was the thought within it. He spoke very little; he only said he was thirsty, and he seemed full of wonder at something.

He lay in wonderment, then stretched himself, and died.

5

AN OLD ACQUAINTANCE

Our division had been out in the field. The work in hand was accomplished: we had cut a way through the forest, and each day we were expecting from headquarters orders for our return to the fort. Our division of fieldpieces was stationed at the top of a steep mountain-crest which was terminated by the swift mountain-river Mechik, and had to command the plain that stretched before us. Here and there on this picturesque plain, out of the reach of gunshot, now and then, especially at evening, groups of mounted mountaineers showed themselves, attracted by curiosity to ride up and view the Russian camp.

The evening was clear, mild, and fresh, as it is apt to be in December in the Caucasus; the sun was setting behind the steep chain of the mountains at the left, and threw rosy rays upon the tents scattered over the slope, upon the soldiers moving about, and upon our two guns, which seemed to crane their necks as they rested motionless on the earthwork two paces from us. The infantry picket, stationed on the knoll at the left, stood in perfect silhouette against the light of the sunset; no less distinct were the stacks of muskets, the form of the sentry, the groups of soldiers, and the smoke of the smouldering campfire.

At the right and left of the slope, on the black, sodden earth, the tents gleamed white; and behind the tents, black, stood the bare trunks of the platan forest, which rang with the incessant sound of axes, the crackling of the bonfires, and the crashing of the trees as they fell under the axes. The bluish smoke arose from tobacco-pipes on all sides, and vanished in the transparent blue of the frosty sky. By the tents and on the lower ground around the arms rushed the Cossacks, dragoons, and artillerists, with great galloping and snorting of horses as they returned from getting water. It began to freeze; all sounds were heard with extraordinary distinctness, and one could see an immense distance across the plain through the clear, rare atmosphere. The groups of the enemy, their curiosity at seeing the soldiers satisfied, quietly galloped off across the fields, still yellow with the golden corn-stubble, toward their auls, or villages, which were visible beyond the forest, with the tall posts of the cemeteries and the smoke rising in the air.

Our tent was pitched not far from the guns on a place high and dry, from which we had a remarkably extended view. Near the tent, on a cleared space, around the battery itself, we had our games of skittles, or chushki. The obliging soldiers had made for us rustic benches and tables. On account of all these amusements, the artillery officers, our comrades, and a few infantry men liked to gather of an evening around our battery, and the place came to be called the club.

As the evening was fine, the best players had come, and we were amusing ourselves with skittles. Ensign D., Lieutenant O., and myself had played two games in succession; and to the common satisfaction and amusement of all the spectators, officers, soldiers, and servants who were watching us from their tents, we had twice carried the winning party on our backs from one end of the ground to the other. Especially droll was the situation of the huge fat Captain S., who, puffing and smiling good-naturedly, with legs dragging on the ground, rode pickaback on the feeble little Lieutenant O.

When it grew somewhat later, the servants brought three

glasses of tea for the six men of us, and not a spoon; and we who had finished our game came to the plaited settees.

There was standing near them a small bow-legged man, a stranger to us, in a sheepskin jacket, and a papakha, or Circassian cap, with a long overhanging white crown. As soon as we came near where he stood, he took a few irresolute steps, and put on his cap; and several times he seemed to make up his mind to come to meet us, and then stopped again. But after deciding, probably, that it was impossible to remain irresolute, the stranger took off his cap, and, going in a circle around us, approached Captain S.

'Ah, Guskantinli, how is it, old man?' said S., still smiling good-naturedly, under the influence of his ride.

Guskantni, as S. called him, instantly replaced his cap, and made a motion as though to thrust his hands into the pockets of his jacket; but on the side toward me there was no pocket in the jacket, and his small red hand fell into an awkward position. I felt a strong desire to make out who this man was (was he a yunker, or a degraded officer?), and, not realizing that my gaze (that is, the gaze of a strange officer) disconcerted him, I continued to stare at his dress and appearance.

I judged that he was about thirty. His small, round, grey eyes had a sleepy expression, and at the same time gazed calmly out from under the dirty white lambskin of his cap, which hung down over his face. His thick, irregular nose, standing out between his sunken cheeks, gave evidence of emaciation that was the result of illness, and not natural. His restless lips, barely covered by a sparse, soft, whitish moustache, were constantly changing their shape as though they were trying to assume now one expression, now another. But all these expressions seemed to be endless, and his face retained one predominating expression of timidity and fright. Around his thin neck, where the veins stood out, was tied a green woollen scarf tucked into his jacket, his fur jacket, or polushubok, was worn bare, short, and had dog-fur sewed on the collar and on the false pockets. The trousers were checkered, of ash-grey colour, and his sapogi had short, unblacked military bootlegs.

'I beg of you, do not disturb yourself,' said I when he for the second time, timidly glancing at me, had taken off his cap.

He bowed to me with an expression of gratitude, replaced his hat, and, drawing from his pocket a dirty chintz tobacco-pouch with lacings, began to roll a cigarette.

I myself had not been long a yunker, an elderly yunker; and as I was incapable, as yet, of being good-naturedly serviceable to my younger comrades, and without means, I well knew all the moral difficulties of this situation for a proud man no longer young, and I sympathized with all men who found themselves in such a situation, and I endeavoured to make clear to myself their character and rank, and the tendencies of their intellectual peculiarities, in order to judge of the degree of their moral sufferings. This yunker or degraded officer, judging by his restless eyes and that intentionally constant variation of expression which I noticed in him, was a man very far from stupid, and extremely egotistical, and therefore much to be pitied.

Captain S. invited us to play another game of skittles, with the stakes to consist, not only of the usual pickaback ride of the winning party, but also of a few bottles of red wine, rum, sugar, cinnamon, and cloves for the mulled wine which that winter, on account of the cold, was greatly popular in our division.

Guskantini, as S. again called him, was also invited to take part; but before the game began, the man, struggling between gratification because he had been invited and a certain timidity, drew Captain S. aside, and began to say something in a whisper. The good-natured captain punched him in the ribs with his big, fat hand, and replied, loud enough to be heard:

'Not at all, old fellow, I assure you.'

When the game was over, and that side in which the stranger whose rank was so low had taken part, had come out winners, and it fell to his lot to ride on one of our officers, Ensign D., the ensign grew red in the face: he went to the little divan and offered the stranger a cigarette by way of a compromise.

While they were ordering the mulled wine, and in the steward's tent were heard assiduous preparations on the part of Nikfta, who had sent an orderly for cinnamon and cloves, and the shadow of his back was alternately lengthening and shortening on the dingy sides of the tent, we men, seven in all, sat around on the benches; and while we took turns in drinking tea from the three glasses, and gazed out over the plain, which was now beginning to glow in the twilight, we talked and laughed over the various incidents of the game.

The stranger in the fur jacket took no share in the conversation, obstinately refused to drink the tea which I several times offered him, and as he sat there on the ground in Tatar fashion, occupied himself in making cigarettes of fine-cut tobacco, and smoking them one after another, evidently not so much for his own satisfaction as to give himself the appearance of a man with something to do. When it was remarked that the summons to return was expected on the morrow, and that there might be an engagement, he lifted himself on his knees, and, addressing Captain B. only, said that he had been at the adjutant's, and had himself written the order for the return on the next day. We all said nothing while he was speaking; and notwithstanding the fact that he was so bashful, we begged him to repeat this most interesting piece of news. He repeated what he had said, adding only that he had been staying at the adjutant's (since he made it his home there) when the order came.

'Look here, old fellow, if you are not telling us false, I shall have to go to my company and give some orders for tomorrow,' said Captain S.

'No...why...it may be, I am sure,' stammered the stranger, but suddenly stopped, and, apparently feeling himself affronted, contracted his brows, and, muttering something between his teeth, again began to roll a cigarette. But the fine-cut tobacco in his chintz pouch began to show signs of giving out, and he asked S. to lend him a little cigarette.

We kept on for a considerable time with that monotonous military chatter which everyone who has ever been on an expedition will appreciate; all of us, with one and the same expression, complaining of the dulness and length of the expedition, in one and the same fashion sitting in judgment on our superiors, and all of us likewise, as we had done many times before, praising one comrade, pitying another, wondering how much this one had gained, how much that one had lost, and so on, and so on.

'Here, fellows, this adjutant of ours is completely broken up,' said Captain S. 'At headquarters he was everlastingly on the winning side; no matter whom he sat down with, he'd rake in everything: but now for two months past he has been losing all the time. The present expedition hasn't been lucky for him. I think he has got away with two thousand silver rubles and five hundred rubles' worth of articles,—the carpet that he won at Mukhin's, Nikitin's pistols, Sada's gold watch which Vorontsof gave him. He has lost it all.'

'The truth of the matter in his case,' said Lieutenant O., 'was that he used to cheat everybody; it was impossible to play with him.'

'He cheated everyone, but now it's all gone up in his pipe;' and here Captain S. laughed good-naturedly. 'Our friend Guskof here lives with him. He hasn't quite lost HIM yet: that's so, isn't it, old fellow?' he asked, addressing Guskof.

Guskof tried to laugh. It was a melancholy, sickly laugh, which completely changed the expression of his countenance. Till this moment it had seemed to me that I had seen and known this man before; and, besides the name Guskof, by which Captain S. called him, was familiar to me; but how and when I had seen and known him, I actually could not remember.

'Yes,' said Guskof, incessantly putting his hand to his moustaches, but instantly dropping it again without touching them. 'Pavel Dmitrievitch's luck has been against him in this expedition, such a veine de malheur' he added in a careful but pure French pronunciation, again giving me to think that I had seen him, and seen him often, somewhere. 'I know Pavel Dmitrievitch very well. He has great confidence in me,' he proceeded to say; 'he and I are old friends; that is, he is fond of me,' he explained, evidently fearing that it might be taken as presumption for him to claim old friendship with the adjutant. 'Pavel Dmitrievitch plays admirably; but now, strange as it may seem, it's all up with him, he is just about perfectly ruined; la chance a tourne,' he added, addressing himself particularly to me.

At first we had listened to Guskof with condescending attention; but as soon as he made use of that second French phrase, we all involuntarily turned from him.

'I have played with him a thousand times, and we agreed then that it was strange,' said Lieutenant O., with peculiar emphasis on the word STRANGE. 'I never once won a ruble from him. Why was it, when I used to win of others?'

'Pavel Dmitrievitch plays admirably: I have known him for a long time,' said I. In fact, I had known the adjutant for several years; more than once I had seen him in the full swing of a game, surrounded by officers, and I had remarked his handsome, rather gloomy and always passionless calm face, his deliberate Malo-Russian pronunciation, his handsome belongings and horses, his bold, manly figure, and above all his skill and self-restraint in carrying on the game accurately and agreeably. More than once, I am sorry to say, as I looked at his plump white hands with a diamond ring on the index-finger, passing out one card after another, I grew angry with that ring, with his white hands, with the whole of the adjutant's person, and evil thoughts on his account arose in my mind. But as I afterwards reconsidered the matter coolly, I persuaded myself that he played more skilfully than all with whom he happened to play: the more so, because as I heard his general observations concerning the game,—how one ought not to back out when one had laid the smallest stake, how one ought not to leave off in certain cases as the first rule for honest men, and so forth, and so forth,—it was evident that he was always on the winning side merely from the fact that he played more sagaciously and coolly than the rest of us. And now it seemed that this self-reliant, careful player had been stripped not only of his money but of his effects, which marks the lowest depths of loss for an officer.

'He always had devilish good luck with me,' said Lieutenant O. 'I made a vow never to play with him again.'

'What a marvel you are, old fellow!' said S., nodding at me, and addressing O. 'You lost three hundred silver rubles, that's what you lost to him.'

'More than that,' said the lieutenant savagely.

'And now you have come to your senses; it is rather late in the day, old man, for the rest of us have known for a long time that he was the cheat of the regiment,' said S., with difficulty restraining his laughter, and feeling very well satisfied with his fabrication. 'Here is Guskof right here,—he FIXES his cards for him. That's the reason of the friendship between them, old man' and Captain S., shaking all over, burst out into such a hearty 'ha, ha, ha!' that he spilt the glass of mulled wine which he was holding in his hand. On Guskof's pale emaciated face there showed something like a colour; he opened his mouth several times, raised his hands to his moustaches, and once more dropped them to his side where the pockets should have been, stood up, and then sat down again, and finally in an unnatural voice said to S.: 'It's no joke, Nikolai Ivanovitch, for you to say such things before people who don't know me and who see me in this unlined jacket...because—' His voice failed him, and again his small red hands with their dirty nails went from his jacket to his face, touching his moustache, his hair, his nose, rubbing his eyes, or needlessly scratching his cheek.

'As to saying that, everybody knows it, old fellow,' continued S., thoroughly satisfied with his jest, and not heeding Guskof's complaint. Guskof was still trying to say something; and placing the palm of his right hand on his left knee in a most unnatural position, and gazing at S., he had an appearance of smiling contemptuously.

'No,' said I to myself, as I noticed that smile of his, 'I have not only seen him, but have spoken with him somewhere.'

'You and I have met somewhere,' said I to him when, under the influence of the common silence, S.'s laughter began to calm down. Guskof's mobile face suddenly lighted up, and his eyes, for the first time with a truly joyous expression, rested upon me.

'Why, I recognized you immediately,' he replied in French. 'In '48 I had the pleasure of meeting you quite frequently in Moscow at my sister's.'

I had to apologize for not recognizing him at first in that costume and in that new garb. He arose, came to me, and with his moist hand irresolutely and weakly seized my hand, and sat down by me. Instead of looking at me, though he apparently seemed so glad to see me, he gazed with an expression of unfriendly bravado at the officers.

Either because I recognized in him a man whom I had met a few years before in a dresscoat in a parlour, or because he was suddenly raised in his own opinion by the fact of being recognized, at all events it seemed to me that his face and even his motions completely changed: they now expressed lively intelligence, a childish self-satisfaction in the consciousness of such intelligence, and a certain contemptuous indifference; so that I confess, notwithstanding the pitiable position in which he found himself, my old acquaintance did not so much excite sympathy in me as it did a sort of unfavourable sentiment.

I now vividly remembered our first meeting. In 1848, while I was staying at Moscow, I frequently went to the house of Ivashin, who from childhood had been an old friend of mine. His wife was an agreeable hostess, a charming woman, as everybody said; but she never pleased me.... The winter that I knew her, she often spoke with hardly concealed pride of her brother, who had shortly before completed his course, and promised to be one of the most fashionable and popular young men in the best society of Petersburg. As I knew by reputation the father of the Guskofs, who was very rich and had a distinguished position, and as I knew also the sister's ways, I felt some prejudice against meeting the young man. One evening when I was at Ivashin's, I saw a short, thoroughly pleasant-looking young man, in a black coat, white vest and necktie. My host hastened to make me acquainted with him. The young man, evidently dressed for a ball, with his cap in his hand, was standing before Ivashin, and was eagerly but politely arguing with him about a common friend of ours, who had distinguished himself at the time of the Hungarian campaign. He said that this acquaintance was not at all a hero or a man born for war, as was said of him, but was simply a clever and cultivated man. I recollect, I took part in the argument against Guskof, and went to the extreme of declaring also that intellect and cultivation always bore an inverse relation to bravery; and I recollect how Guskof pleasantly and cleverly pointed out to me that bravery was necessarily the result of intellect and a decided degree of development,—a statement which I, who considered myself an intellectual and cultivated man, could not in my heart of hearts agree with.

I recollect that towards the close of our conversation Madame Ivashina introduced me to her brother; and he, with a condescending smile, offered me his little hand on which he had not yet had time to draw his kid gloves, and weakly and irresolutely pressed my hand as he did now. Though I had been prejudiced against Guskof, I could not help granting that he was in the right, and agreeing with his sister that he was really a clever and agreeable young man, who ought to have great success in society. He was extraordinarily neat, beautifully dressed, and fresh, and had affectedly modest manners, and a thoroughly youthful, almost childish appearance, on account of which you could not help excusing his expression of self-sufficiency, though it modified the impression of his high-mightiness caused by his intellectual face and especially his smile. It is said that he had great success that winter with the high-born ladies of Moscow. As I saw him at his sister's I could only infer how far this was true by the feeling of pleasure and contentment constantly excited in me by his youthful appearance and by his sometimes indiscreet anecdotes. He and I met half a dozen times, and talked a good deal; or, rather, he talked a good deal, and I listened. He spoke for the most part in French, always with a good accent, very fluently and ornately; and he had the skill of drawing others gently and politely into the conversation. As a general thing, he behaved toward all, and toward me, in a somewhat supercilious manner, and I felt that he was perfectly right in this way of treating people. I always feel that way in regard to men who are firmly convinced that they ought to treat me superciliously, and who are comparative strangers to me.

Now, as he sat with me, and gave me his hand, I keenly recalled in him that same old haughtiness of expression; and it seemed to me that he did not properly appreciate his position of official inferiority, as, in the presence of the officers, he asked me what I had been doing in all that time, and how I happened to be there. In spite of the fact that I invariably made my replies in Russian, he kept putting his questions in French, expressing himself as before in remarkably correct language. About himself he said fluently that after his unhappy, wretched story (what the story was, I did not know, and he had not yet told me), he had been three months under arrest, and then had been sent to the Caucasus to the N. regiment, and now had been serving three years as a soldier in that regiment.

'You would not believe,' said he to me in French, 'how much I have to suffer in these regiments from the society of the officers. Still it is a pleasure to me, that I used to know the adjutant of whom we were just speaking: he is a good man—it's a fact,' he remarked condescendingly. 'I live with him, and that's something of a relief for me. Yes, my dear, the days fly by, but they aren't all alike,' he added; and suddenly hesitated, reddened, and stood up, as he caught sight of the adjutant himself coming toward us.

'It is such a pleasure to meet such a man as you,' said Guskof to me in a whisper as he turned from me. 'I should like very, very much, to have a long talk with you.'

I said that I should be very happy to talk with him, but in reality I confess that Guskof excited in me a sort of dull pity that was not akin to sympathy.

I had a presentiment that I should feel a constraint in a private conversation with him; but still I was anxious to learn from him several things, and, above all, why it was, when his father had been so rich, that he was in poverty, as was evident by his dress and appearance.

The adjutant greeted us all, including Guskof, and sat down by me in the seat which the cashiered officer had just vacated. Pavel Dmitrievitch, who had always been calm and leisurely, a genuine gambler, and a man of means, was now very different from what he had been in the flowery days of his success; he seemed to be in haste to go somewhere, kept constantly glancing at everybody, and it was not five minutes before he proposed to Lieutenant O., who had sworn off from playing, to set up a small faro-bank. Lieutenant O. refused, under the pretext of having to attend to his duties, but in reality because, as he knew that the adjutant had few possessions and little money left, he did not feel himself justified in risking his three hundred rubles against a hundred or even less which the adjutant might stake.

'Well, Pavel Dmitrievitch,' said the lieutenant, anxious to avoid a repetition of the invitation, 'is it true, what they tell us, that we return tomorrow?'

'I don't know,' replied the adjutant. 'Orders came to be in readiness; but if it's true, then you'd better play a game. I would wager my Kabarda cloak.'

'No, today already'

'It's a grey one, never been worn; but if you prefer, play for money. How is that?'

'Yes, but...I should be willing—pray don't think that'...said Lieutenant O., answering the implied suspicion; 'but as there may be a raid or some movement, I must go to bed early.'

The adjutant stood up, and, thrusting his hands into his pockets, started to go across the grounds. His face assumed its ordinary expression of coldness and pride, which I admired in him.

'Won't you have a glass of mulled wine?' I asked him.

'That might be acceptable,' and he came back to me; but Guskof politely took the glass from me, and handed it to the adjutant, striving at the same time not to look at him. But as he did not notice the tent-rope, he stumbled over it, and fell on his hand, dropping the glass.

'What a bungler!' exclaimed the adjutant, still holding out his hand for the glass. Everybody burst out laughing, not excepting Guskof, who was rubbing his hand on his sore knee, which he had somehow struck as he fell. 'That's the way the bear waited on the hermit,' continued the adjutant. 'It's the way he waits on me every day. He has pulled up all the tent-pins; he's always tripping up.'

Guskof, not hearing him, apologized to us, and glanced toward me with a smile of almost noticeable melancholy, as though saying that I alone could understand him. He was pitiable to see; but the adjutant, his protector, seemed, on that very account, to be severe on his messmate, and did not try to put him at his ease.

'Well, you're a graceful lad! Where did you think you were going?'

'Well, who can help tripping over these pins, Pavel Dmitrievitch?' said Guskof. 'You tripped over them yourself the other day.'

'I, old man,—I am not of the rank and file, and such gracefulness is not expected of me.'

'He can be lazy,' said Captain S., keeping the ball rolling, 'but low- rank men have to make their legs fly.'

'Ill-timed jest,' said Guskof, almost in a whisper, and casting down his eyes. The adjutant was evidently vexed with his messmate; he listened with inquisitive attention to every word that he said.

'He'll have to be sent out into ambuscade again,' said he, addressing S., and pointing to the cashiered officer.

'Well, there'll be some more tears,' said S., laughing. Guskof no longer looked at me, but acted as though he were going to take some tobacco from his pouch, though there had been none there for some time.

'Get ready for the ambuscade, old man,' said S., addressing him with shouts of laughter. 'Today the scouts have brought the news, there'll be an attack on the camp tonight, so it's necessary to designate the trusty lads.' Guskof's face showed a fleeting smile as though he were preparing to make some reply, but several times he cast a supplicating look at S.

'Well, you know I have been, and I'm ready to go again if I am sent,' he said hastily.

'Then you'll be sent.'

'Well, I'll go. Isn't that all right?'

'Yes, as at Arguna, you deserted the ambuscade and threw away your gun,' said the adjutant; and turning from him he began to tell us the orders for the next day.

As a matter of fact, we expected from the enemy a cannonade of the camp that night, and the next day some sort of diversion.

While we were still chatting about various subjects of general interest, the adjutant, as though from a sudden and unexpected impulse, proposed to Lieutenant O. to have a little game. The lieutenant most unexpectedly consented; and, together with S. and the ensign, they went off to the adjutant's tent, where there was a folding green table with cards on it. The captain, the commander of our division, went to our tent to sleep; the other gentlemen also separated, and Guskof and I were left alone. I was not mistaken, it was really very uncomfortable for me to have a tete-a-tete with him; I arose involuntarily, and began to promenade up and down on the battery. Guskof walked in silence by my side, hastily and awkwardly wheeling around so as not to delay or incommode me.

'I do not annoy you?' he asked in a soft, mournful voice. So far as I could see his face in the dim light, it seemed to me deeply thoughtful and melancholy.

'Not at all,' I replied; but as he did not immediately begin to speak, and as I did not know what to say to him, we walked in silence a considerably long time.

The twilight had now absolutely changed into dark night; over the black profile of the mountains gleamed the bright evening heat-lightning; over our heads in the light-blue frosty sky twinkled the little stars; on all sides gleamed the ruddy flames of the smoking watch-fires; near us, the white tents stood out in contrast to the frowning blackness of our earth-works. The light from the nearest watch-fire, around which our servants, engaged in quiet conversation, were warming themselves, occasionally flashed on the brass of our heavy guns, and fell on the form of the sentry, who, wrapped in his cloak, paced with measured tread along the battery.

'You cannot imagine what a delight it is for me to talk with such a man as you are,' said Guskof, although as yet he had not spoken a word to me. 'Only one who had been in my position could appreciate it.'

I did not know how to reply to him, and we again relapsed into silence, although it was evident that he was anxious to talk and have me listen to him.

'Why were you...why did you suffer this?' I inquired at last, not being able to invent any better way of breaking the ice.

'Why, didn't you hear about this wretched business from Metenin?'

'Yes, a duel, I believe; I did not hear much about it,' I replied. 'You see, I have been for some time in the Caucasus.'

'No, it wasn't a duel, but it was a stupid and horrid story. I will tell you all about it, if you don't know. It happened that the same year that I met you at my sister's I was living at Petersburg. I must tell you I had then what they call une position dans le monde,—a position good enough if it was not brilliant. Mon pere me donnait ten thousand par an. In '49 I was promised a place in the embassy at Turin; my uncle on my mother's side had influence, and was always ready to do a great deal for me. That sort of thing is all past now. J'etais recu dans la meilleure societe de Petersburg; I might have aspired to any girl in the city. I was well educated, as we all are who come from the school, but was not especially cultivated; to be sure, I read a good deal afterwards, mais j'avais surtout, you know, ce jargon du monde, and, however it came about, I was looked upon as a leading light among the young men of Petersburg. What raised me more than all in common estimation, c'est cette liaison avec Madame D., about which a great deal was said in Petersburg; but I was frightfully young at that time, and did not prize these advantages very highly. I was simply young and stupid. What more did I need? Just then that Metenin had some notoriety—'

And Guskof went on in the same fashion to relate to me the history of his misfortunes, which I will omit, as it would not be at all interesting.

'Two months I remained under arrest,' he continued, 'absolutely alone; and what thoughts did I not have during that time? But, you know, when it was all over, as though every tie had been broken with the past, then it became easier for me. Mon pere,—you have heard tell of him, of course, a man of iron will and strong convictions,—il m'a desherite, and broken off all intercourse with me. According to his convictions he had to do as he did, and I don't blame him at all. He was consistent. Consequently, I have not taken a step to induce him to change his mind. My sister was abroad. Madame D. is the only one who wrote to me when I was released, and she sent me assistance; but you understand that I could not accept it, so that I had none of those little things which make one's position a little easier, you know,—books, linen, food, nothing at all. At this time I thought things over and over, and began to look at life with different eyes. For instance, this noise, this society gossip about me in Petersburg, did not interest me, did not flatter me; it all seemed to me ridiculous. I felt that I myself had been to blame; I was young and indiscreet; I had spoiled my career, and I only thought how I might get into the right track again. And I felt that I had strength and energy enough for it. After my arrest, as I told you, I was sent here to the Caucasus to the N. regiment.

'I thought,' he went on to say, all the time becoming more and more animated,—'I thought that here in the Caucasus, la vie de camp, the simple, honest men with whom I should associate, and war and danger, would all admirably agree with my mental state, so that I might begin a new life. They will see me under fire. I shall make myself liked; I shall be respected for my real self,—the cross—non-commissioned officer; they will relieve me of my fine; and I shall get up again, et vous savez avec ce prestige du malheur! But, quel desenchantement! You can't imagine how I have been deceived! You know what sort of men the officers of our regiment are.'

He did not speak for some little time, waiting, as it appeared, for me to tell him that I knew the society of our officers here was bad; but I made him no reply. It went against my grain that he should expect me, because I knew French, forsooth, to be obliged to take issue with the society of the officers, which, during my long residence in the Caucasus, I had had time enough to appreciate fully, and for which I had far higher respect than for the society from which Mr. Guskof had sprung. I wanted to tell him so, but his position constrained me.

'In the N. regiment the society of the officers is a thousand times worse than it is here,' he continued. 'I hope that it is saying a good deal; j'espere que c'est beaucoup dire; that is, you cannot imagine what it is. I am not speaking of the yunkers and the soldiers. That is horrible, it is so bad. At first they received me very kindly, that is absolutely the truth; but when they saw that I could not help despising them, you know, in these inconceivably small circumstances, they saw that I was a man absolutely different, standing far above them, they got angry with me, and began to put various little humiliations on me. You haven't an idea what I had to suffer. Then this forced relationship with the yunkers, and especially with the small means that I had—I lacked everything; I had only what my sister used to send me. And here's a proof for you! As much as it made me suffer, I with my character, avec ma fierte j'ai ecris a mon pere, begged him to send me something. I understand how living four years of such a life may make a man like our cashiered Dromof who drinks with soldiers, and writes notes to all the officers asking them to loan him three rubles, and signing it, tout a vous, dromof. One must have such a character as I have, not to be mired in the least by such a horrible position.'

For some time he walked in silence by my side.

'Have you a cigarette?' he asked me.

'And so I stayed right where I was? Yes. I could not endure it physically, because, though we were wretched, cold, and ill-fed, I lived like a common soldier, but still the officers had some sort of consideration for me. I had still some prestige that they regarded. I wasn't sent out on guard nor for drill. I could not have stood that. But morally my sufferings were frightful; and especially because I didn't see any escape from my position. I wrote to my uncle, begged him to get me transferred to my present regiment, which, at least, sees some service; and I thought that here Pavel Dmitrievitch, qui est le fils de l'intendant de mon pere, might be of some use to me. My uncle did this for me; I was transferred. After that regiment this one seemed to me a collection of chamberlains. Then Pavel Dmitrievitch was here; he knew who I was, and I was splendidly received. At my uncle's request—a Guskof, vous savez; but I forgot that with these men without cultivation and undeveloped, they can't appreciate a man, and show him marks of esteem, unless he has that aureole of wealth, of friends; and I noticed how, little by little, when they saw that I was poor, their behaviour to me showed more and more indifference until they have come almost to despise me. It is horrible, but it is absolutely the truth.

'Here I have been in action, I have fought, they have seen me under fire,' he continued; 'but when will it all end? I think, never. And my strength and energy have already begun to flag. Then I had imagined la guerre, la vie de camp; but it isn't at all what I see, in a sheepskin jacket, dirty linen, soldier's boots, and you go out in ambuscade, and the whole night long lie in the ditch with some Antonof reduced to the ranks for drunkenness, and any minute from behind the bush may come a rifle-shot and hit you or Antonof,—it's all the same which. That is not bravery; it's horrible, c'est affreux, it's killing!'

'Well, you can be promoted a non-commissioned officer for this campaign, and next year an ensign,' said I.

'Yes, it may be: they promised me that in two years, and it's not up yet. What would those two years amount to, if I knew any one! You can imagine this life with Pavel Dmitrievitch; cards, low jokes, drinking all the time; if you wish to tell anything that is weighing on your mind, you would not be understood, or you would be laughed at: they talk with you, not for the sake of sharing a thought, but to get something funny out of you. Yes, and so it has gone—in a brutal, beastly way, and you are always conscious that you belong to the rank and file; they always make you feel that. Hence you can't realize what an enjoyment it is to talk a coeur ouvert to such a man as you are.'

I had never imagined what kind of a man I was, and consequently I did not know what answer to make him.

'Will you have your lunch now?' asked Nikita at this juncture, approaching me unseen in the darkness, and, as I could perceive, vexed at the presence of a guest. 'Nothing but curd dumplings, there's none of the roast beef left.'

'Has the captain had his lunch yet?'

'He went to bed long ago,' replied Nikita, gruffly, 'According to my directions, I was to bring you lunch here and your brandy.' He muttered something else discontentedly, and sauntered off to his tent. After loitering a while longer, he brought us, nevertheless, a lunch-case; he placed a candle on the lunch-case, and shielded it from the wind with a sheet of paper. He brought a saucepan, some mustard in a jar, a tin dipper with a handle, and a bottle of absinthe. After arranging these things, Nikita lingered around us for some moments, and looked on as Guskof and I were drinking the liquor, and it was evidently very distasteful to him. By the feeble light shed by the candle through the paper, amid the encircling darkness, could be seen the seal-skin cover of the lunch-case, the supper arranged upon it, Guskof's sheepskin jacket, his face, and his small red hands which he used in lifting the patties from the pan. Everything around us was black; and only by straining the sight could be seen the dark battery, the dark form of the sentry moving along the breastwork, on all sides the watchfires, and on high the ruddy stars.

Guskof wore a melancholy, almost guilty smile as though it

were awkward for him to look into my face after his confession. He drank still another glass of liquor, and ate ravenously, emptying the saucepan.

'Yes; for you it must be a relief all the same,' said I, for the sake of saying something,—'your acquaintance with the adjutant. He is a very good man, I have heard.'

'Yes,' replied the cashiered officer, 'he is a kind man; but he can't help being what he is, with his education, and it is useless to expect it.'

A flush seemed suddenly to cross his face. 'You remarked his coarse jest this evening about the ambuscade;' and Guskof, though I tried several times to interrupt him, began to justify himself before me, and to show that he had not run away from the ambuscade, and that he was not a coward as the adjutant and Capt. S. tried to make him out.

'As I was telling you,' he went on to say, wiping his hands on his jacket, 'such people can't show any delicacy toward a man, a common soldier, who hasn't much money either. That's beyond their strength. And here recently, while I haven't received anything at all from my sister, I have been conscious that they have changed toward me. This sheepskin jacket, which I bought of a soldier, and which hasn't any warmth in it, because it's all worn off' (and here he showed me where the wool was gone from the inside), 'it doesn't arouse in him any sympathy or consideration for my unhappiness, but scorn, which he does not take pains to hide. Whatever my necessities may be, as now when I have nothing to eat except soldiers' gruel, and nothing to wear,' he continued, casting down his eyes, and pouring out for himself still another glass of liquor, 'he does not even offer to lend me some money, though he knows perfectly well that I would give it back to him; but he waits till I am obliged to ask him for it. But you appreciate how it is for me to go to him. In your case I should say, square and fair, vous etes audessus de cela, mon cher, je n'ai pas le sou.

And you know,' said he, looking straight into my eyes with an expression of desperation, 'I am going to tell you, square and fair, I am in a terrible situation: pouvez-vous me preter dix rubles argent? My sister ought to send me some by the mail, et mon pere—'

'Why, most willingly,' said I, although, on the contrary, it was trying and unpleasant, especially because the evening before, having lost at cards, I had left only about five rubles in Nikita's care. 'In a moment,' said I, arising, 'I will go and get it at the tent.'

'No, by and by: ne vous derangez pas.'

Nevertheless, not heeding him, I hastened to the closed tent, where stood my bed, and where the captain was sleeping.

'Aleksei Ivanuitch, let me have ten rubles, please, for rations,' said I to the captain, shaking him.

'What! have you been losing again? But this very evening, you were not going to play any more,' murmured the captain, still half asleep.

'No, I have not been playing; but I want the money; let me have it, please.'

'Makatiuk!' shouted the captain to his servant, 'hand me my bag with the money.'

'Hush, hush!' said I, hearing Guskof's measured steps near the tent.

'What? Why hush?'

'Because that cashiered fellow has asked to borrow it of me. He's right there.'

'Well, if you knew him, you wouldn't let him have it,' remarked the captain. 'I have heard about him. He's a dirty, low-life fellow.'

Nevertheless, the captain gave me the money, ordered his man to put away the bag, pulled the flap of the tent neatly to, and, again saying, 'If you only knew him, you wouldn't let him have it,' drew his head down under the coverlet. 'Now you owe me thirty-two, remember,' he shouted after me.

When I came out of the tent, Guskof was walking near the

settees; and his slight figure, with his crooked legs, his shapeless cap, his long white hair, kept appearing and disappearing in the darkness, as he passed in and out of the light of the candles. He made believe not to see me.

I handed him the money. He said 'Merci,' and, crumpling the bank-bill, thrust it into his trousers pocket.

'Now I suppose the game is in full swing at the adjutant's,' he began immediately after this.

'Yes, I suppose so.'

'He's a wonderful player, always bold, and never backs out. When he's in luck, it's fine; but when it does not go well with him, he can lose frightfully. He has given proof of that. During this, expedition, if you reckon his valuables, he has lost more than fifteen hundred rubles. But, as he played discreetly before, that officer of yours seemed to have some doubts about his honour.'

'Well, that's because he...Nikita, haven't we any of that red Kavkas wine left?' I asked, very much enlivened by Guskof's conversational talent. Nikita still kept muttering; but he brought us the red wine, and again looked on angrily as Guskof drained his glass. In Guskof's behaviour was noticeable his old freedom from constraint. I wished that he would go as soon as possible; it seemed as if his only reason for not going was because he did not wish to go immediately after receiving the money. I said nothing.

'How could you, who have means, and were under no necessity, simply *de gaiete de coeur*, make up your mind to come and serve in the Caucasus? That's what I don't understand,' said he to me.

I endeavoured to explain this act of renunciation, which seemed so strange to him.

'I can imagine how disagreeable the society of those officers—men without any comprehension of culture—must be for you. You could not understand each other. You see, you might live ten years, and not see anything, and not hear about anything, except cards, wine, and gossip about rewards and campaigns.'

It was unpleasant for me, that he wished me to put myself on a par with him in his position; and, with absolute honesty, I assured him that I was very fond of cards and wine, and gossip about campaigns, and that I did not care to have any better comrades than those with whom I was associated. But he would not believe me.

'Well, you may say so,' he continued; 'but the lack of women's society—I mean, of course, femmes comme il faut—is that not a terrible deprivation? I don't know what I would give now to go into a parlour, if only for a moment, and to have a look at a pretty woman, even though it were through a crack.'

He said nothing for a little, and drank still another glass of the red wine.

'Oh, my God, my God! If it only might be our fate to meet again, somewhere in Petersburg, to live and move among men, among ladies!'

He drank up the dregs of the wine still left in the bottle, and when he had finished it he said: 'akh! PARDON, maybe you wanted some more. It was horribly careless of me. However, I suppose I must have taken too much, and my head isn't very strong. There was a time when I lived on Morskaia Street, au rez-de-chaussee, and had marvellous apartments, furniture, you know, and I was able to arrange it all beautifully, not so very expensively though; my father, to be sure, gave me porcelains, flowers, and silver—a wonderful lot. Le matin je sortais, visits, 5 heures regulierement. I used to go and dine with her; often she was alone. Il faut avouer que c'etait une femme ravissante! You didn't know her at all, did you?'

'No.'

'You see, there was such high degree of womanliness in her, and such tenderness, and what love! Lord! I did not know how to appreciate my happiness then. We would return after the theatre, and have a little supper together. It was never dull where she was, toujours gaie, toujours aimante. Yes, and I had never imagined what rare happiness it was. Et j'ai beaucoup a me reprocher in regard to her. Je l'ai fait souffrir et souvent. I was outrageous. AKH! What a marvellous time that was! Do I bore you?'

'No, not at all.'

'Then I will tell you about our evenings. I used to go—that stairway, every flower-pot I knew,—the door-handle, all was so lovely, so familiar; then the vestibule, her room…No, it will never, never come back to me again! Even now she writes to me: if you will let me, I will show you her letters. But I am not what I was; I am ruined; I am no longer worthy of her….Yes, I am ruined for ever. Je suis casse. There's no energy in me, no pride, nothing—nor even any rank. Yes, I am ruined; and no one will ever appreciate my sufferings. Every one is indifferent. I am a lost man. Never any chance for me to rise, because I have fallen morally…into the mire—I have fallen.'…

At this moment there was evident in his words a genuine, deep despair: he did not look at me, but sat motionless.

'Why are you in such despair?' I asked.

'Because I am abominable. This life has degraded me, all that was in me, all is crushed out. It is not by pride that I hold out, but by abjectness: there's no dignite dans le malheur. I am humiliated every moment; I endure it all; I got myself into this abasement. This mire has soiled me. I myself have become coarse; I have forgotten what I used to know; I can't speak French any more; I am conscious that I am base and low. I cannot tear myself away from these surroundings, indeed I cannot. I might have been a hero: give me a regiment, gold epaulets, a trumpeter, but to march in the ranks with some wild Anton Bondarenko or the like, and feel that between me and him there was no difference at all—that he might be killed or I might be killed—all the same, that thought is maddening. You understand how horrible it is to think that some ragamuffin may kill me, a man who has thoughts and feelings, and that it would make no difference if alongside of me some Antonof were killed—a being not different from an animal—and that it might easily happen that I and not this Antonof were killed, which is always UNE FATALITE for every lofty and good man. I know that they call me a coward: grant that I am a coward, I certainly am a coward, and can't be anything else. Not only am I a coward, but I am in my way a low and despicable man. Here I have just been borrowing money of you, and you have the right to despise me. No, take back your money.' And he held out to me the crumpled bank-bill. 'I want you to have a good opinion of me.' He covered his face with his hands, and burst into tears. I really did not know what to say or do.

'Calm yourself,' I said to him. 'You are too sensitive; don't take everything so to heart; don't indulge in self-analysis, look at things more simply. You yourself say that you have character. Keep up good heart, you won't have long to wait,' I said to him, but not very consistently, because I was much stirred both by a feeling of sympathy and a feeling of repentance, because I had allowed myself mentally to sin in my judgment of a man truly and deeply unhappy.

'Yes,' he began, 'if I had heard even once, at the time when I was in that hell, one single word of sympathy, of advice, of friendship—one humane word such as you have just spoken, perhaps I might have calmly endured all; perhaps I might have struggled, and been a soldier. But now this is horrible...When I think soberly, I long for death. Why should I love my despicable life and my own self, now that I am ruined for all that is worthwhile in the world? And at the least danger, I suddenly, in spite of myself, begin to pray for my miserable life, and to watch over it as though it were precious, and I cannot, je ne puis pas, control myself. That is, I could,' he continued again after a minute's silence, 'but this is too hard work for me, a monstrous work, when I am alone.

With others, under special circumstances, when you are going into action, I am brave, j'ai fait mes epreuves, because I am vain and proud: that is my failing, and in presence of others...Do you know, let me spend the night with you: with us, they will play all night long; it makes no difference, anywhere, on the ground.'

While Nikita was making the bed, we got up, and once more began to walk up and down in the darkness on the battery. Certainly Guskof's head must have been very weak, because two glasses of liquor and two of wine made him dizzy. As we got up and moved away from the candles, I noticed that he again thrust the ten-ruble bill into his pocket, trying to do so without my seeing it. During all the foregoing conversation, he had held it in his hand. He continued to reiterate how he felt that he might regain his old station if he had a man such as I were to take some interest in him.

We were just going into the tent to go to bed when suddenly a cannon-ball whistled over us, and buried itself in the ground not far from us. So strange it was,—that peacefully sleeping camp, our conversation, and suddenly the hostile cannon-ball which flew from God knows where, the midst of our tents,—so strange that it was some time before I could realize what it was. Our sentinel, Andreief, walking up and down on the battery, moved toward me.

'Ha! he's crept up to us. It was the fire here that he aimed at,' said he.

'We must rouse the captain,' said I, and gazed at Guskof.

He stood cowering close to the ground, and stammered, trying to say, 'Th-that's th-the ene-my's...f-f-fire—th-that's—hidi.' Further he could not say a word, and I did not see how and where he disappeared so instantaneously.

In the captain's tent a candle gleamed; his cough, which always troubled him when he was awake, was heard; and he himself soon appeared, asking for a linstock to light his little pipe.

'What does this mean, old man?' he asked with a smile. 'Aren't they willing to give me a little sleep tonight? First it's you with your cashiered friend, and then it's Shamyl. What shall we do, answer him or not? There was nothing about this in the instructions, was there?'

'Nothing at all. There he goes again,' said I. 'Two of them!'

Indeed, in the darkness, directly in front of us, flashed two fires, like two eyes; and quickly over our heads flew one cannon-ball and one heavy shell. It must have been meant for us, coming with a loud and penetrating hum. From the neighbouring tents the soldiers hastened. You could hear them hawking and talking and stretching themselves.

'Hist! the fuse sings like a nightingale,' was the remark of the artillerist.

'Send for Nikita,' said the captain with his perpetually benevolent smile. 'Nikita, don't hide yourself, but listen to the mountain nightingales.'

'Well, your honour,' said Nikita, who was standing near the captain, 'I have seen them—these nightingales. I am not afraid of 'em; but here was that stranger who was here, he was drinking up your red wine. When he heard how that shot dashed by our tents, and the shell rolled by, he cowered down like some wild beast.'

'However, we must send to the commander of the artillery,' said the captain to me, in a serious tone of authority, 'and ask whether we shall reply to the fire or not. It will probably be nothing at all, but still it may. Have the goodness to go and ask him. Have a horse saddled. Do it as quickly as possible, even if you take my Polkan.'

In five minutes they brought me a horse, and I galloped off to the commander of the artillery. 'Look you, return on foot,' whispered the punctilious captain, 'else they won't let you through the lines.'

It was half a verst to the artillery commander's, the whole road ran between the tents. As soon as I rode away from our fire, it became so black that I could not see even the horse's ears, but only the watch-fires, now seeming very near, now very far off, as they gleamed into my eyes. After I had ridden some distance, trusting to the intelligence of the horse whom I allowed free rein, I began to distinguish the white four-cornered tents and then the black tracks of the road. After a half-hour, having asked my way three times, and twice stumbled over the tent-stakes, causing each time a volley of curses from the tents, and twice been detained by the sentinels, I reached the artillery commander's. While I was on the way, I heard two more cannon shot in the direction of our camp; but the projectiles did not reach to the place where the headquarters were. The artillery commander ordered not to reply to the firing, the more as the enemy did not remain in the same place; and I went back, leading the horse by the bridle, making my way on foot between the infantry tents. More than once I delayed my steps, as I went by some soldier's tent where a light was shining, and some merry-andrew was telling a story; or I listened to some educated soldier reading from some book while the whole division overflowed the tent, or hung around it, sometimes interrupting the reading with various remarks; or I simply listened to the talk about the expedition, about the fatherland, or about their chiefs.

As I came around one of the tents of the third battalion, I heard Guskof's rough voice: he was speaking hilariously and rapidly. Young voices replied to him, not those of soldiers, but of gay gentlemen. It was evidently the tent of some yunker or sergeant-major. I stopped short.

'I've known him a long time,' Guskof was saying. 'When I lived in Petersburg, he used to come to my house often; and I went to his. He moved in the best society.'

'Whom are you talking about?' asked the drunken voice.

'About the prince,' said Guskof. 'We were relatives, you see, but, more than all, we were old friends. It's a mighty good thing, you know, gentlemen, to have such an acquaintance. You see he's fearfully rich. To him a hundred silver rubles is a mere bagatelle. Here, I just got a little money out of him, enough to last me till my sister sends.'

'Let's have some.'

'Right away, Savelitch, my dear,' said Guskof, coming to the door of the tent, 'here's ten rubles for you: go to the sutler, get two bottles of Kakhetinski. Anything else, gentlemen? What do you say?' and Guskof, with unsteady gait, with dishevelled hair, without his hat, came out of the tent. Throwing open his jacket, and thrusting his hands into the pockets of his trousers, he stood at the door of the tent. Though he was in the light, and I in darkness; I trembled with fear lest he should see me, and I went on, trying to make no noise.

'Who goes there?' shouted Guskof after me in a thoroughly drunken voice. Apparently, the cold took hold of him. 'Who the devil is going off with that horse?'

I made no answer, and silently went on my way.

6

DOES A MAN NEED MUCH LAND?

AN elder sister came to visit her younger sister in the country. The elder was married to a tradesman in town, the younger to a peasant in the village. As the sisters sat over their tea talking, the elder began to boast of the advantages of town life: saying how comfortably they lived there, how well they dressed, what fine clothes her children wore what good things they ate and drank, and how she went to the theatre, promenades, and entertainments.

The younger sister was piqued, and in turn disparage the life of a tradesman, and stood up for that of a peasant.

'I would not change my way of life for yours,' said she. We may live roughly, but at least we are free from anxiety. You live in better style than we do but though you often earn more than you need, you are very likely to lose all you have. You know the proverb, 'Loss and gain are brothers twain.' It often happens that people who are wealthy one day are begging their bread the next. Our way is safer. Though a peasant's life is not a fat one, it is a long one. We shall never grow rich, but we shall always have enough to eat.'

The elder sister said sneeringly: 'Enough? Yes, if you like to share with the pigs and the calves! What do you know of elegance or manners! However much your good man may slave, you will die as you are living—on a dung heap—and your children the same.'

'Well, what of that?' replied the younger. 'Of course our work is rough and coarse. But, on the other hand, it is sure; and we need not bow to any one. But you, in your towns, are surrounded by temptations; today all may be right, but tomorrow the Evil One may tempt your husband with cards, wine, or women, and all will go to ruin. Don't such things happen often enough?'

Pahóm, the master of the house, was lying on the top of the oven, and he listened to the women's chatter.

'It is perfectly true,' thought he. 'Busy as we are from childhood tilling mother earth, we peasants have no time to let any nonsense settle in our heads. Our only trouble is that we haven't land enough. If I had plenty of land, I shouldn't fear the Devil himself!'

The women finished their tea, chatted a while about dress, and then cleared away the tea-things and lay down to sleep.

But the Devil had been sitting behind the oven, and had heard all that was said. He was pleased that the peasant's wife had led her husband into boasting, and that he had said that if he had plenty of land he would not fear the Devil himself.

'All right,' thought the Devil. 'We will have a tussle. I'll give you land enough; and by means of that land I will get you into my power.'

Close to the village there lived a lady, a small landowner, who had an estate of about three hundred acres. She had always lived on good terms with the peasants, until she engaged as her steward an old soldier, who took to burdening the people with fines. However careful Pahóm tried to be, it happened again and again that now a horse of his got among the lady's oats, now a cow strayed into her garden, now his calves found their way into her meadows—and he always had to pay a fine.

Pahóm paid up, but grumbled, and, going home in a temper, was rough with his family. All through that summer, Pahóm had much trouble because of this steward; and he was even glad when winter came and the cattle had to be stabled. Though he grudged the fodder when they could no longer graze on the pasture-land, at least he was free from anxiety about them.

In the winter the news got about that the lady was going to sell her land, and that the keeper of the inn on the high road was bargaining for it. When the peasants heard this they were very much alarmed.

'Well,' thought they, 'if the innkeeper gets the land, he will worry us with fines worse than the lady's steward. We all depend on that estate.'

So the peasants went on behalf of their Commune and asked the lady not to sell the land to the innkeeper offering her a better price for it themselves. The lady agreed to let them have it. Then the peasants tried to arrange for the Commune to buy the whole estate so that it might be held by them all in common. They met twice to discuss it, but could not settle the matter; the Evil One sowed discord among them, and they could not agree. So they decided to buy the land individually, each according to his means; and the lady agreed to this plan as she had to the other.

Presently Pahóm heard that a neighbour of his was buying fifty acres, and that the lady had consented to accept one half in cash and to wait a year for the other half. Pahóm felt envious

'Look at that,' thought he, 'the land is all being sold, and I shall get none of it.' So he spoke to his wife.

'Other people are buying,' said he, 'and we must also buy twenty acres or so. Life is becoming impossible. That steward is simply crushing us with his fines.'

So they put their heads together and considered how they could manage to buy it. They had one hundred roubles laid by. They sold a colt, and one half of their bees; hired out one of their sons as a labourer, and took his wages in advance; borrowed the rest from a brother-in-law, and so scraped together half the purchase money.

Having done this, Pahóm chose out a farm of forty acres, some of it wooded, and went to the lady to bargain for it. They came to an agreement, and he shook hands with her upon it, and paid her a deposit in advance. Then they went to town and signed the deeds; he paying half the price down, and undertaking to pay the remainder within two years.

So now Pahóm had land of his own. He borrowed seed, and sowed it on the land he had bought. The harvest was a good one, and within a year he had managed to pay off his debts both to the lady and to his brother-in-law. So he became a landowner, ploughing and sowing his own land, making hay on his own land, cutting his own trees, and feeding his cattle on his own pasture. When he went out to plough his fields, or to look at his growing corn, or at his grass-meadows, his heart would fill with joy. The grass that grew and the flowers that bloomed there, seemed to him unlike any that grew elsewhere. Formerly, when he had passed by that land it had appeared the same as any other land, but now it seemed quite different.

So Pahóm was well-contented, and everything would have been right if the neighbouring peasants would only not have trespassed on his corn-fields and meadows. He appealed to them most civilly, but they still went on: now the Communal herdsmen would let the village cows stray into his meadows; then horses from the night pasture would get among his corn. Pahóm turned them out again and again, and forgave their owners, and for a long time he forbore from prosecuting any one. But at last he lost patience and complained to the District Court. He knew it was the peasants' want of land, and no evil intent on their part, that caused the trouble; but he thought:

'I cannot go on overlooking it, or they will destroy all I have. They must be taught a lesson.'

So he had them up, gave them one lesson, and then another, and two or three of the peasants were fined. After a time Pahóm's neighbours began to bear him a grudge for this, and would now and then let their cattle on to his land on purpose. One peasant even got into Pahóm's wood at night and cut down five young lime trees for their bark. Pahóm passing through the wood one day noticed something white. He came nearer, and saw the stripped trunks lying on the ground, and close by stood the stumps, where the trees had been. Pahóm was furious.

'If he had only cut one here and there it would have been bad enough,' thought Pahóm, 'but the rascal has actually cut down a whole clump. If I could only find out who did this, I would pay him out.'

He racked his brains as to who it could be. Finally he decided: 'It must be Simon—no one else could have done it.' So he went to Simon's homestead to have a look round, but he found nothing, and only had an angry scene. However, he now felt more certain than ever that Simon had done it, and he lodged a complaint. Simon was summoned. The case was tried, and re-tried, and at the end of it all Simon was acquitted, there being no evidence against him. Pahóm felt still more aggrieved, and let his anger loose upon the Elder and the Judges.

'You let thieves grease your palms,' said he. 'If you were honest folk yourselves, you would not let a thief go free.'

So Pahóm quarrelled with the Judges and with his neighbours. Threats to burn his building began to be uttered. So though Pahóm had more land, his place in the Commune was much worse than before.

About this time a rumour got about that many people were moving to new parts.

'There's no need for me to leave my land,' thought Pahóm. 'But some of the others might leave our village and then there would be more room for us. I would take over their land myself, and make my estate a bit bigger. I could then live more at ease. As it is, I am still too cramped to be comfortable.

One day Pahóm was sitting at home, when a peasant, passing through the village, happened to call in. He was allowed to stay the night, and supper was given him. Pahóm had a talk with this peasant and asked him where he came from. The stranger answered that he came from beyond the Volga, where he had been working. One word led to another, and the man went on to say that many people were settling in those parts. He told how some people from his village had settled there. They had joined the Commune, and had had twenty-five acres per man granted them. The land was so good, he said, that the rye sown on it grew as high as a horse, and so thick that five cuts of a sickle made a sheaf. One peasant, he said, had brought nothing with him but his bare hands, and now he had six horses and two cows of his own.

Pahóm's heart kindled with desire. He thought: 'Why should I suffer in this narrow hole, if one can live so well elsewhere? I will sell my land and my homestead here, and with the money I will start afresh over there and get everything new. In this crowded place one is always having trouble. But I must first go and find out all about it myself.'

Towards summer he got ready and started. He went down the Volga on a steamer to Samára, then walked another three hundred miles on foot, and at last reached the place. It was just as the stranger had said. The peasants had plenty of land: every man had twenty-five acres of Communal land given him for his use, and any one who had money could buy, besides, at two shillings an acres much good freehold land as he wanted.

Having found out all he wished to know, Pahóm returned home as autumn came on, and began selling off his belongings. He sold his land at a profit, sold his homestead and all his cattle, and withdrew from membership of the Commune. He only waited till the spring, and then started with his family for the new settlement.

As soon as Pahóm and his family arrived at their new abode, he applied for admission into the Commune of a large village. He stood treat to the Elders, and obtained the necessary documents. Five shares of Communal land were given him for his own and his sons' use: that is to say—125 acres (not all together but in different fields) besides the use of the Communal pasture. Pahóm put up the buildings he needed, and bought cattle. Of the Communal land alone he had three times as much as at his former home, and the land was good corn-land. He was ten times better off than he had been. He had plenty of arable land and pasturage, and could keep as many head of cattle as he liked.

At first, in the bustle of building and settling down, Pahóm was pleased with it all, but when he got used to it he began to think that even here he had not enough land. The first year, he sowed wheat on his share of the Communal land, and had a good crop. He wanted to go on sowing wheat, but had not enough Communal land for the purpose, and what he had already used was not available; for in those parts wheat is only sown on virgin soil or on fallow land. It is sown for one or two years, and then the land lies fallow till it is again overgrown with prairie grass. There were many who wanted such land, and there was not enough for all; so that people quarrelled about it. Those who were better off, wanted it for growing wheat, and those who were poor, wanted it to let to dealers, so that they might raise money to pay their taxes. Pahóm wanted to sow more wheat; so he rented land from a dealer for a year. He sowed much wheat and had a fine crop, but the land was too far from the village—the wheat had to be carted more than ten miles. After a time Pahóm noticed that some peasant-dealers were living on separate farms, and were growing wealthy; and he thought: 'If I were to buy some freehold land, and have a homestead on it, it would be a different thing altogether. Then it would all be nice and compact.'

The question of buying freehold land recurred to him again and again.

He went on in the same way for three years: renting land and sowing wheat. The seasons turned out well and the crops were good, so that he began to lay money by. He might have gone on living contentedly, but he grew tired of having to rent other people's land every year, and having to scramble for it. Wherever there was good land to be had, the peasants would rush for it and it was taken up at once, so that unless you were sharp about it you got none. It happened in the third year that he and a dealer together rented a piece of pasture land from some peasants; and they had already ploughed it up, when there was some dispute, and the peasants went to law about it, and things fell out so that the labour was all lost.

'If it were my own land,' thought Pahóm, 'I should be independent, and there would not be all this unpleasantness.'

So Pahóm began looking out for land which he could buy; and he came across a peasant who had bought thirteen hundred acres, but having got into difficulties was willing to sell again cheap. Pahóm bargained and haggled with him, and at last they settled the price at 1,500 roubles, part in cash and part to be paid later. They had all but clinched the matter, when a passing dealer happened to stop at Pahóm's one day to get a feed for his horses. He drank tea with Pahóm, and they had a talk. The dealer said that he was just returning from the land of the Bashkírs, far away, where he had bought thirteen thousand acres of land, all for 1,000 roubles. Pahóm questioned him further, and the tradesman said:

'All one need do is to make friends with the chiefs. I gave away about one hundred roubles, worth of dressing-gowns and carpets, besides a case of tea, and I gave wine to those who would drink it; and I got the land for less than twopence an acre. And he showed Pahóm the title-deeds, saying:

'The land lies near a river, and the whole prairie is virgin soil.'

Pahóm plied him with questions, and the tradesman said:
'There is more land there than you could cover if you walked a year, and it all belongs to the Bashkírs. They are as simple as sheep,

and land can be got almost for nothing.'

'There now,' thought Pahóm, 'with my one thousand roubles, why should I get only thirteen hundred acres, and saddle myself with a debt besides. If I take it out there, I can get more than ten times as much for the money.'

Pahóm inquired how to get to the place, and as soon as the tradesman had left him, he prepared to go there himself. He left his wife to look after the homestead, and started on his journey taking his man with him. They stopped at a town on their way, and bought a case of tea, some wine, and other presents, as the tradesman had advised. On and on they went until they had gone more than three hundred miles, and on the seventh day they came to a place where the Bashkírs had pitched their tents. It was all just as the tradesman had said. The people lived on the steppes, by a river, in felt-covered tents. They neither tilled the ground, nor ate bread. Their cattle and horses grazed in herds on the steppe. The colts were tethered behind the tents, and the mares were driven to them twice a day. The mares were milked, and from the milk kumiss was made. It was the women who prepared kumiss, and they also made cheese. As far as the men were concerned, drinking kumiss and tea, eating mutton, and playing on their pipes, was all they cared about. They were all stout and merry, and all the summer long they never thought of doing any work. They were quite ignorant, and knew no Russian, but were good-natured enough.

As soon as they saw Pahóm, they came out of their tents and gathered round their visitor. An interpreter was found, and Pahóm told them he had come about some land. The Bashkírs seemed very glad they took Pahóm and led him into one of the best tents, where they made him sit on some down-cushions placed on a carpet, while they sat round him. They gave him tea and kumiss, and had a sheep killed, and gave him mutton to eat. Pahóm took presents out of his cart and distributed them among the Bashkírs, and divided amongst them the tea. The Bashkírs were delighted. They talked a great deal among themselves, and then told the interpreter to translate.

'They wish to tell you,' said the interpreter, 'that they like you, and that it is our custom to do all we can to please a guest and to repay him for his gifts. You have given us presents, now tell us which of the things we possess please you best, that we may present them to you.'

'What pleases me best here,' answered Pahóm 'is your land. Our land is crowded, and the soil is exhausted; but you have plenty of land and it is good land. I never saw the like of it.'

The interpreter translated. The Bashkírs talked among themselves for a while. Pahóm could not understand what they were saying, but saw that they were much amused, and that they shouted and laughed. Then they were silent and looked at Pahóm while the interpreter said:

'They wish me to tell you that in return for your presents they will gladly give you as much land as you want. You have only to point it out with your hand and it is yours.'

The Bashkírs talked again for a while and began to dispute. Pahóm asked what they were disputing about, and the interpreter told him that some of them thought they ought to ask their Chief about the land and not act in his absence, while others thought there was no need to wait for his return.

While the Bashkírs were disputing, a man in a large fox-fur cap appeared on the scene. They all became silent and rose to their feet. The interpreter said, 'This is our Chief himself.'

Pahóm immediately fetched the best dressing-gown and five pounds of tea, and offered these to the Chief. The Chief accepted them, and seated himself in the place of honour. The Bashkírs at once began telling him something. The Chief listened for a while, then made a sign with his head for them to be silent, and addressing himself to Pahóm, said in Russian:

'Well, let it be so. Choose whatever piece of land you like; we have plenty of it.'

'How can I take as much as I like?' thought Pahóm. 'I must get a deed to make it secure, or else they may say, 'It is yours,' and afterwards may take it away again.'

'Thank you for your kind words,' he said aloud. 'You have much land, and I only want a little. But I should like to be sure which bit is mine. Could it not be measured and made over to me? Life and death are in God's hands. You good people give it to me, but your children might wish to take it away again.'

'You are quite right,' said the Chief. 'We will make it over to you.'

'I heard that a dealer had been here,' continued Pahóm, 'and that you gave him a little land, too, and signed title-deeds to that effect. I should like to have it done in the same way.'

The Chief understood.

'Yes,' replied he, 'that can be done quite easily. We have a scribe, and we will go to town with you and have the deed properly sealed.'

'And what will be the price?' asked Pahóm.

'Our price is always the same: one thousand roubles a day.'

Pahóm did not understand.

'A day? What measure is that? How many acres would that be?'

'We do not know how to reckon it out,' said the Chief. 'We sell it by the day. As much as you can go round on your feet in a day is yours, and the price is one thousand roubles a day.'

Pahóm was surprised.

'But in a day you can get round a large tract of land,' he said.

The Chief laughed.

'It will all be yours!' said he. 'But there is one condition: If you don't return on the same day to the spot whence you started, your money is lost.'

'But how am I to mark the way that I have gone?'

'Why, we shall go to any spot you like, and stay there. You must start from that spot and make your round, taking a spade with you. Wherever you think necessary, make a mark. At every turning, dig a hole and pile up the turf; then afterwards we will go round with a plough from hole to hole. You may make as large a circuit as you please, but before the sun sets you must return to the place you started from. All the land you cover will be yours.'

Pahóm was delighted. It was decided to start early next morning. They talked a while, and after drinking some more kumiss and eating some more mutton, they had tea again, and then the night came on. They gave Pahóm a feather-bed to sleep on, and the Bashkírs dispersed for the night, promising to assemble the next morning at daybreak and ride out before sunrise to the appointed spot.

Pahóm lay on the feather-bed, but could not sleep. He kept thinking about the land.

'What a large tract I will mark off!' thought he. 'I can easily do thirty-five miles in a day. The days are long now, and within a circuit of thirty-five miles what a lot of land there will be! I will sell the poorer land, or let it to peasants, but I'll pick out the best and farm it. I will buy two ox teams, and hire two more labourers. About a hundred and fifty acres shall be plough-land, and I will pasture cattle on the rest.'

Pahóm lay awake all night, and dozed off only just before dawn. Hardly were his eyes closed when he had a dream. He thought he was lying in that same tent, and heard somebody chuckling outside. He wondered who it could be, and rose and went out and he saw the Bashkír Chief sitting in front of the tent holding his sides and rolling about with laughter. Going nearer to the Chief, Pahóm asked: 'What are you laughing at?' But he saw that it was no longer the Chief, but the dealer who had recently stopped at his house and had told him about the land. Just as

Pahóm was going to ask, 'Have you been here long?' he saw that it was not the dealer, but the peasant who had come up from the Volga, long ago, to Pahóm's old home. Then he saw that it was not the peasant either, but the Devil himself with hoofs and horns sitting there and chuckling, and before him lay a man barefoot, prostrate on the ground, with only trousers and a shirt on. And Pahóm dreamt that he looked more attentively to see what sort of a man it was that was lying there, and he saw that the man was dead and that it was himself! He awoke horror-struck.

'What things one does dream,' thought he.

Looking round he saw through the open door that the dawn was breaking.

'It's time to wake them up,' thought he. 'We ought to be starting.'

He got up, roused his man (who was sleeping in his cart), bade him harness; and went to call the Bashkírs.

'It's time to go to the steppe to measure the land,' he said.

The Bashkírs rose and assembled, and the Chief came too. Then they began drinking kumiss again, and offered Pahóm some tea, but he would not wait.

'If we are to go, let us go. It is high time,' said he.

The Bashkírs got ready and they all started: some mounted on horses, and some in carts. Pahóm drove in his own small cart with his servant, and took a spade with him. When they reached the steppe, the morning red was beginning to kindle. They ascended a hillock (called by the Bashkírs a shikhan) and dismounting from their carts and their horses, gathered in one spot. The Chief came up to Pahóm and stretching out his arm towards the plain:

'See,' said he, 'all this, as far as your eye can reach, is ours. You may have any part of it you like.'

Pahóm's eyes glistened: it was all virgin soil, as flat as the palm of your hand, as black as the seed of a poppy, and in the hollows different kinds of grasses grew breast high.

The Chief took off his fox-fur cap, placed it on the ground and said:

'This will be the mark. Start from here, and return here again. All the land you go round shall be yours.'

Pahóm took out his money and put it on the cap. Then he took off his outer coat, remaining in his sleeveless under-coat. He unfastened his girdle and tied it tight below his stomach, put a little bag of bread into the breast of his coat, and tying a flask of water to his girdle, he drew up the tops of his boots, took the spade from his man, and stood ready to start. He considered for some moments which way he had better go—it was tempting everywhere.

'No matter,' he concluded, 'I will go towards the rising sun.'

He turned his face to the east, stretched himself and waited for the sun to appear above the rim.

'I must lose no time,' he thought, 'and it is easier walking while it is still cool.'

The sun's rays had hardly flashed above the horizon, before Pahóm, carrying the spade over his shoulder went down into the steppe.

Pahóm started walking neither slowly nor quickly. After having gone a thousand yards he stopped, dug a hole, and placed pieces of turf one on another to make it more visible. Then he went on; and now that he had walked off his stiffness he quickened his pace. After a while he dug another hole.

Pahóm looked back. The hillock could be distinctly seen in the sunlight, with the people on it, and the glittering tyres of the cart-wheels. At a rough guess Pahóm concluded that he had walked three miles. It was growing warmer; he took off his under-coat, flung it across his shoulder, and went on again. It had grown quite warm now; he looked at the sun, it was time to think of breakfast.

'The first shift is done, but there are four in a day, and it is too soon yet to turn. But I will just take off my boots,' said he to himself.

He sat down, took off his boots, stuck them into his girdle, and went on. It was easy walking now.

'I will go on for another three miles,' thought he, 'and then turn to the left. This spot is so fine, that it would be a pity to lose it. The further one goes, the better the land seems.'

He went straight on for a while, and when he looked round, the hillock was scarcely visible and the people on it looked like black ants, and he could just see something glistening there in the sun.

'Ah,' thought Pahóm, 'I have gone far enough in this direction, it is time to turn. Besides I am in a regular sweat, and very thirsty.'

He stopped, dug a large hole, and heaped up pieces of turf. Next he untied his flask, had a drink, and then turned sharply to the left. He went on and on; the grass was high, and it was very hot.

Pahóm began to grow tired: he looked at the sun and saw that it was noon.

'Well,' he thought, 'I must have a rest.'

He sat down, and ate some bread and drank some water; but he did not lie down, thinking that if he did he might fall asleep. After sitting a little while, he went on again. At first he walked easily: the food had strengthened him; but it had become terribly hot, and he felt sleepy; still he went on, thinking: 'An hour to suffer, a life-time to live.'

He went a long way in this direction also, and was about to turn to the left again, when he perceived a damp hollow: 'It would be a pity to leave that out,' he thought. 'Flax would do well there.' So he went on past the hollow, and dug a hole on the other side of it before he turned the corner. Pahóm looked towards the hillock. The heat made the air hazy: it seemed to be quivering, and through the haze the people on the hillock could scarcely be seen.

'Ah!' thought Pahóm, 'I have made the sides too long; I must make this one shorter.' And he went along the third side stepping faster. He looked at the sun: it was nearly half way to the horizon, and he had not yet done two miles of the third side of the square. He was still ten miles from the goal.

'No,' he thought, 'though it will make my land lop-sided, I must hurry back in a straight line now. I might go too far, and as it is I have a great deal of land.'

So Pahóm hurriedly dug a hole, and turned straight towards the hillock.

Pahóm went straight towards the hillock, but he now walked with difficulty. He was done up with the heat, his bare feet were cut and bruised, and his legs began to fail. He longed to rest, but it was impossible if he meant to get back before sunset. The sun waits for no man, and it was sinking lower and lower.

'Oh dear,' he thought, 'if only I have not blundered trying for too much! What if I am too late?'

He looked towards the hillock and at the sun. He was still far from his goal, and the sun was already near the rim

Pahóm walked on and on; it was very hard walking, but he went quicker and quicker. He pressed on, but was still far from the place. He began running, threw away his coat, his boots, his flask, and his cap, and kept only the spade which he used as a support.

'What shall I do,' he thought again, 'I have grasped too much, and ruined the whole affair. I can't get there before the sun sets.'

And this fear made him still more breathless. Pahóm went on running, his soaking shirt and trousers stuck to him, and his mouth was parched. His breast was working like a blacksmith's bellows, his heart was beating like a hammer, and his legs were giving way as if they did not belong to him. Pahóm was seized with terror lest he should die of the strain.

Though afraid of death, he could not stop. 'After having run all that way they will call me a fool if I stop now,' thought he. And he ran on and on, and drew near and heard the Bashkírs yelling and shouting to him, and their cries inflamed his heart still more.

He gathered his last strength and ran on.

The sun was close to the rim, and cloaked in mist looked large, and red as blood. Now, yes now, it was about to set! The sun was quite low, but he was also quite near his aim. Pahóm could already see the people on the hillock waving their arms to hurry him up. He could see the fox-fur cap on the ground, and the money on it, and the Chief sitting on the ground holding his sides. And Pahóm remembered his dream.

'There is plenty of land,' thought he, 'but will God let me live on it? I have lost my life, I have lost my life! I shall never reach that spot!'

Pahóm looked at the sun, which had reached the earth: one side of it had already disappeared. With all his remaining strength he rushed on, bending his body forward so that his legs could hardly follow fast enough to keep him from falling. Just as he reached the hillock it suddenly grew dark. He looked up—the sun had already set! He gave a cry: 'All my labour has been in vain,' thought he, and was about to stop, but he heard the Bashkírs still shouting, and remembered that though to him, from below, the sun seemed to have set, they on the hillock could still see it. He took a long breath and ran up the hillock. It was still light there. He reached the top and saw the cap. Before it sat the Chief laughing and holding his sides. Again Pahóm remembered his dream, and he uttered a cry: his legs gave way beneath him, he fell forward and reached the cap with his hands.

'Ah, that's a fine fellow!' exclaimed the Chief 'He has gained much land!'

Pahóm's servant came running up and tried to raise him, but he saw that blood was flogging from his mouth. Pahóm was dead!

The Bashkírs clicked their tongues to show their pity.

His servant picked up the spade and dug a grave long enough for Pahóm to be in, and buried him in it. Six feet from his head to his heels was all he needed.

7

A SPARK NEGLECTED BURNS THE HOUSE

There once lived in a village a peasant named Iván Stcherbakóf. He was comfortably off, in the prime of life, the best worker in the village, and had three sons all able to work. The eldest was married, the second about to marry, and the third was a big lad who could mind the horses and was already beginning to plough. Ivan's wife was an able and thrifty woman, and they were fortunate in having a quiet, hard-working daughter-in-law. There was nothing to prevent Iván and his family from living happily. They had only one idle mouth to feed; that was Iván's old father, who suffered from asthma and had been lying ill on the top of the brick oven for seven years. Iván had all he needed: three horses and a colt, a cow with a calf, and fifteen sheep. The women made all the clothing for the family, besides helping in the fields, and the men tilled the land. They always had grain enough of their own to last over beyond the next harvest and sold enough oats to pay the taxes and meet their other needs. So Iván and his children might have lived quite comfortably had it not been for a feud between him and his next-door neighbour, Limping Gabriel, the son of Gordéy Ivánof.

As long as old Gordéy was alive and Iván's father was still able to manage the household, the peasants lived as neighbours should.

If the women of either house happened to want a sieve or a tub, or the men required a sack, or if a cart-wheel got broken and could not be mended at once, they used to send to the other house, and helped each other in neighbourly fashion. When a calf strayed into the neighbour's thrashing-ground they would just drive it out, and only say, 'Don't let it get in again; our grain is lying there.' And such things as locking up the barns and outhouses, hiding things from one another, or backbiting were never thought of in those days.

That was in the fathers' time. When the sons came to be at the head of the families, everything changed.

It all began about a trifle.

Iván's daughter-in-law had a hen that began laying rather early in the season, and she started collecting its eggs for Easter. Every day she went to the cart-shed, and found an egg in the cart; but one day the hen, probably frightened by the children, flew across the fence into the neighbour's yard and laid its egg there. The woman heard the cackling, but said to herself: 'I have no time now; I must tidy up for Sunday. I'll fetch the egg later on.' In the evening she went to the cart, but found no egg there. She went and asked her mother-in-law and brother-in-law whether they had taken the egg. 'No,' they had not; but her youngest brother-in-law, Tarás, said: 'Your Biddy laid its egg in the neighbour's yard. It was there she was cackling, and she flew back across the fence from there.'

The woman went and looked at the hen. There she was on the perch with the other birds, her eyes just closing ready to go to sleep. The woman wished she could have asked the hen and got an answer from her.

Then she went to the neighbour's, and Gabriel's mother came out to meet her.

'What do you want, young woman?'

'Why, Granny, you see, my hen flew across this morning. Did she not lay an egg here?'

'We never saw anything of it. The Lord be thanked, our own hens started laying long ago. We collect our own eggs and have no need of other people's! And we don't go looking for eggs in other people's yards, lass!'

The young woman was offended, and said more than she should have done. Her neighbour answered back with interest, and the women began abusing each other. Ivan's wife, who had been to fetch water, happening to pass just then, joined in too. Gabriel's wife rushed out, and began reproaching the young woman with things that had really happened and with other things that never had happened at all. Then a general uproar commenced, all shouting at once, trying to get out two words at a time, and not choice words either.

'You're this!' and 'You're that!' 'You're a thief!' and 'You're a slut!' and 'You're starving your old father-in-law to death!' and 'You're a good-for-nothing!' and so on.

'And you've made a hole in the sieve I lent you, you jade! And it's our yoke you're carrying your pails on—you just give back our yoke!'

Then they caught hold of the yoke, and spilt the water, snatched off one another's shawls, and began fighting. Gabriel, returning from the fields, stopped to take his wife's part. Out rushed Iván and his son and joined in with the rest. Iván was a strong fellow, he scattered the whole lot of them, and pulled a handful of hair out of Gabriel's beard. People came to see what was the matter, and the fighters were separated with difficulty.

That was how it all began.

Gabriel wrapped the hair torn from his beard in a paper, and went to the District Court to have the law of Iván. 'I didn't grow my beard,' said he, 'for pockmarked Iván to pull it out!' And his wife went bragging to the neighbours, saying they'd have Iván condemned and sent to Siberia. And so the feud grew.

The old man, from where he lay on the top of the oven, tried from the very first to persuade them to make peace, but they would not listen. He told them, 'It's a stupid thing you are after, children, picking quarrels about such a paltry matter. Just think! The whole thing began about an egg. The children may have taken it—well, what matter? What's the value of one egg? God sends enough for all! And suppose your neighbour did say an unkind word—put it right; show her how to say a better one! If there has been a fight—well, such things will happen; we're all sinners, but make it up, and let there be an end of it! If you nurse your anger it will be worse for you yourselves.'

But the younger folk would not listen to the old man. They thought his words were mere senseless dotage. Iván would not humble himself before his neighbour.

'I never pulled his beard,' he said, 'he pulled the hair out himself. But his son has burst all the fastenings on my shirt, and torn it....Look at it!'

And Iván also went to law. They were tried by the Justice of the Peace and by the District Court. While all this was going on, the coupling-pin of Gabriel's cart disappeared. Gabriel's womenfolk accused Ivan's son of having taken it. They said: 'We saw him in the night go past our window, towards the cart; and a neighbour says he saw him at the pub, offering the pin to the landlord.'

So they went to law about that. And at home not a day passed without a quarrel or even a fight. The children, too, abused one another, having learnt to do so from their elders; and when the women happened to meet by the river-side, where they went to rinse the clothes, their arms did not do as much wringing as their tongues did nagging, and every word was a bad one.

At first the peasants only slandered one another; but afterwards they began in real earnest to snatch anything that lay handy, and the children followed their example. Life became harder and harder for them. Iván Stcherbakóf and Limping Gabriel kept suing one another at the Village Assembly, and at the District Court, and before the Justice of the Peace until all the judges were tired of them. Now Gabriel got Iván fined or imprisoned; then Iván did as much to Gabriel; and the more they spited each other the angrier they grew—like dogs that attack one another and get more and more furious the longer they fight. You strike one dog from behind, and it thinks it's the other dog biting him, and gets still fiercer. So these peasants: they went to law, and one or other of them was fined or locked up, but that only made them more and more angry with each other. 'Wait a bit,' they said, 'and I'll make you pay for it.' And so it went on for six years. Only the old man lying on the top of the oven kept telling them again and again: 'Children, what are you doing? Stop all this paying back; keep to your work, and don't bear malice—it will be better for you. The more you bear malice, the worse it will be.'

But they would not listen to him.

In the seventh year, at a wedding, Ivan's daughter-in-law held Gabriel up to shame, accusing him of having been caught horse-stealing. Gabriel was tipsy, and unable to contain his anger, gave the woman such a blow that she was laid up for a week; and she was pregnant at the time. Iván was delighted. He went to the magistrate to lodge a complaint. 'Now I'll get rid of my neighbour! He won't escape imprisonment, or exile to Siberia.' But Ivan's wish was not fulfilled. The magistrate dismissed the case. The woman was examined, but she was up and about and showed no sign of any injury. Then Ivan went to the Justice of the Peace, but he referred the business to the District Court. Ivan bestirred himself: treated the clerk and the Elder of the District Court to a gallon of liquor and got Gabriel condemned to be flogged. The sentence was read out to Gabriel by the clerk: 'The Court decrees that the peasant Gabriel Gordéyef shall receive twenty lashes with a birch rod at the District Court.'

Ivan too heard the sentence read, and looked at Gabriel to see how he would take it. Gabriel grew as pale as a sheet, and turned round and went out into the passage. Ivan followed him, meaning to see to the horse, and he overheard Gabriel say, 'Very well! He will have my back flogged: that will make it burn; but something of his may burn worse than that!'

Hearing these words, Ivan at once went back into the Court, and said: 'Upright judges! He threatens to set my house on fire! Listen: he said it in the presence of witnesses!'

Gabriel was recalled. 'Is it true that you said this?'

'I haven't said anything. Flog me, since you have the power. It seems that I alone am to suffer, and all for being in the right, while he is allowed to do as he likes.'

Gabriel wished to say something more, but his lips and his cheeks quivered, and he turned towards the wall. Even the officials were frightened by his looks. 'He may do some mischief to himself or to his neighbour,' thought they.

Then the old Judge said: 'Look here, my men; you'd better be reasonable and make it up. Was it right of you, friend Gabriel, to strike a pregnant woman? It was lucky it passed off so well, but think what might have happened! Was it right? You had better confess and beg his pardon, and he will forgive you, and we will alter the sentence.'

The clerk heard these words, and remarked: 'That's impossible under Statute 117. An agreement between the parties not having been arrived at, a decision of the Court has been pronounced and must be executed.'

But the Judge would not listen to the clerk.

'Keep your tongue still, my friend,' said he. 'The first of all laws is to obey God, Who loves peace.' And the Judge began again to persuade the peasants, but could not succeed. Gabriel would not listen to him.

'I shall be fifty next year,' said he, 'and have a married son, and have never been flogged in my life, and now that pockmarked Ivan has had me condemned to be flogged, and am I to go and ask his forgiveness? No; I've borne enough....Ivan shall have cause to remember me!'

Again Gabriel's voice quivered, and he could say no more, but turned round and went out.

It was seven miles from the Court to the village, and it was getting late when Ivan reached home. He unharnessed his horse, put it up for the night, and entered the cottage. No one was there. The women had already gone to drive the cattle in, and the young fellows were not yet back from the fields. Iván went in, and sat down, thinking. He remembered how Gabriel had listened to the sentence, and how pale he had become, and how he had turned to the wall; and Ivan's heart grew heavy. He thought how he himself would feel if he were sentenced, and he pitied Gabriel. Then he heard his old father up on the oven cough, and saw him sit up, lower his legs, and scramble down. The old man dragged himself slowly to a seat, and sat down. He was quite tired out with the exertion, and coughed a long time till he had cleared his throat. Then, leaning against the table, he said: 'Well, has he been condemned?'

'Yes, to twenty strokes with the rods,' answered Iván.

The old man shook his head.

'A bad business,' said he. 'You are doing wrong, Iván! Ah! it's very bad—not for him so much as for yourself!...Well, they'll flog him: but will that do you any good?'

'He'll not do it again,' said Iván.

'What is it he'll not do again? What has he done worse than you?'

'Why, think of the harm he has done me!' said Iván. 'He nearly killed my wife, and now he's threatening to burn us up. Am I to thank him for it?'

The old man sighed, and said: 'You go about the wide world, Iván, while I am lying on the oven all these years, so you think you see everything, and that I see nothing....Ah, lad! It's you that don't see; malice blinds you. Others' sins are before your eyes, but your own are behind your back. 'He's acted badly!' What a thing to say! If he were the only one to act badly, how could strife exist? Is strife among men ever bred by one alone? Strife is always between two. His badness you see, but your own you don't. If he were bad, but you were good, there would be no strife. Who pulled the hair out of his beard? Who spoilt his haystack? Who dragged him to the law court? Yet you put it all on him! You live a bad life yourself, that's what is wrong! It's not the way I used to live, lad, and it's not the way I taught you. Is that the way his old father and I used to live? How did we live? Why, as neighbours should! If he happened to run out of flour, one of the women would come across: 'Uncle Trol, we want some flour.' 'Go to the barn, dear,' I'd say: 'take what you need.' If he'd no one to take his horses to pasture, 'Go, Iván,' I'd say, 'and look after his horses.' And if I was short of anything, I'd go to him. 'Uncle Gordéy,' I'd say, 'I want so-and-so!' 'Take it Uncle Trol!' That's how it was between us, and we had an easy time of it. But now?...That soldier the other day was telling us about the fight at Plevna (a town in Bulgaria, the scene of fierce and prolonged fighting between the Turks and the Russians in the war of 1877). Why, there's war between you worse than at Plevna! Is that living?...What a sin it is! You are a man and master of the house; it's you who will have to answer. What are you teaching the women and the children? To snarl and snap? Why, the other day your Taráska—that greenhorn—was swearing at neighbour Irena, calling her names; and his mother listened and laughed. Is that right? It is you will have to answer. Think of your soul. Is this all as it should be? You throw a word at me, and I give you two in return; you give me a blow, and I give you two. No, lad! Christ, when He walked on earth, taught us fools something very different....If you get a hard word from any one, keep silent, and his own conscience will accuse him. That is what our Lord taught. If you get a slap, turn the other cheek. 'Here, beat me, if that's what I deserve!' And his own conscience will rebuke him. He will soften, and will listen to you. That's the way He taught us, not to be proud!...Why don't you speak? Isn't it as I say?'

Iván sat silent and listened.

The old man coughed, and having with difficulty cleared his throat, began again: 'You think Christ taught us wrong? Why, it's all for our own good. Just think of your earthly life; are you better off, or worse, since this Plevna began among you? Just reckon up what you've spent on all this law business—what the driving backwards and forwards and your food on the way have cost you! What fine fellows your sons have grown; you might live and get on well; but now your means are lessening. And why? All because of this folly; because of your pride. You ought to be ploughing with your lads, and do the sowing yourself; but the fiend carries you off to the judge, or to some pettifogger or other. The ploughing is not done in time, nor the sowing, and mother earth can't bear properly. Why did the oats fail this year? When did you sow them? When you came back from town! And what did you gain? A burden for your own shoulders....Eh, lad, think of your own business! Work with your boys in the field and at home, and if some one offends you, forgive him, as God wished you to. Then life will be easy, and your heart will always be light.'

Iván remained silent.

'Iván, my boy, hear your old father! Go and harness the roan, and go at once to the Government office; put an end to all this affair there; and in the morning go and make it up with Gabriel in God's name, and invite him to your house for tomorrow's holiday' (it was the eve of the Virgin's Nativity). 'Have tea ready, and get a bottle of vódka and put an end to this wicked business, so that there should not be any more of it in future, and tell the women and children to do the same.'

Iván sighed, and thought, 'What he says is true,' and his heart grew lighter. Only he did not know how, now, to begin to put matters right.

But again the old man began, as if he had guessed what was in Ivan's mind.

'Go, Iván, don't put it off! Put out the fire before it spreads, or it will be too late.'

The old man was going to say more, but before he could do so the women came in, chattering like magpies. The news that Gabriel was sentenced to be flogged, and of his threat to set fire to the house, had already reached them. They had heard all about it and added to it something of their own, and had again had a row, in the pasture, with the women of Gabriel's household. They began telling how Gabriel's daughter-in-law threatened a fresh action: Gabriel had got the right side of the examining magistrate, who would now turn the whole affair upside down; and the schoolmaster was writing out another petition, to the Tsar himself this time, about Iván; and everything was in the petition—all about the coupling-pin and the kitchen-garden—so that half of Iván's homestead would be theirs soon. Iván heard what they were saying, and his heart grew cold again, and he gave up the thought of making peace with Gabriel.

In a farmstead there is always plenty for the master to do. Iván did not stop to talk to the women, but went out to the threshing-floor and to the barn. By the time he had tidied up there, the sun had set and the young fellows had returned from the field. They had been ploughing the field for the winter crops with two horses. Iván met them, questioned them about their work, helped to put everything in its place, set a torn horse-collar aside to be mended, and was going to put away some stakes under the barn, but it had grown quite dusk, so he decided to leave them where they were till next day. Then he gave the cattle their food, opened the gate, let out the horses. Tarás was to take to pasture for the night, and again closed the gate and barred it. 'Now,' thought he, 'I'll have my supper, and then to bed.' He took the horse-collar and entered the hut. By this time he had forgotten about Gabriel and about what his old father had been saying to him. But, just as he took hold of the door-handle to enter the passage, he heard his neighbour on the other side of the fence cursing somebody in a hoarse voice: 'What the devil is he good for?' Gabriel was saying. 'He's only fit to be killed!' At these words all Iván's former bitterness towards his neighbour re-awoke. He stood listening while Gabriel scolded, and, when he stopped, Iván went into the hut.

There was a light inside; his daughter-in-law sat spinning, his wife was getting supper ready, his eldest son was making straps for bark shoes, his second sat near the table with a book, and Tarás was getting ready to go out to pasture the horses for the night. Everything in the hut would have been pleasant and bright, but for that plague—a bad neighbour!

Iván entered, sullen and cross; threw the cat down from the bench, and scolded the women for putting the slop-pail in the wrong place. He felt despondent, and sat down, frowning, to mend the horse-collar. Gabriel's words kept ringing in his ears: his threat at the law court, and what he had just been shouting in a hoarse voice about some one who was 'only fit to be killed.'

His wife gave Tarás his supper, and, having eaten it, Tarás put on an old sheepskin and another coat, tied a sash round his waist, took some bread with him, and went out to the horses. His eldest brother was going to see him off, but Iván himself rose instead, and went out into the porch. It had grown quite dark outside, clouds had gathered, and the wind had risen. Iván went down the steps, helped his boy to mount, started the foal after him, and stood listening while Tarás rode down the village and was there joined by other lads with their horses. Iván waited until they were all out of hearing. As he stood there by the gate he could not get Gabriel's words out of his head: 'Mind that something of yours does not burn worse!'

'He is desperate,' thought Iván. 'Everything is dry, and it's windy weather besides. He'll come up at the back somewhere, set fire to something, and be off. He'll burn the place and escape scot free, the villain!...There now, if one could but catch him in the act, he'd not get off then!' And the thought fixed itself so firmly in his mind that he did not go up the steps but went out into the street and round the corner. I'll just walk round the buildings; who can tell what he's after?' And Iván, stepping softly, passed out of the gate. As soon as he reached the corner, he looked round along the fence, and seemed to see something suddenly move at the opposite corner, as if someone had come out and disappeared again. Iván stopped, and stood quietly, listening and looking. Everything was still; only the leaves of the willows fluttered in the wind, and the straws of the thatch rustled. At first it seemed pitch dark, but, when his eyes had grown used to the darkness, he could see the far corner, and a plough that lay there, and the eaves. He looked a while, but saw no one.

'I suppose it was a mistake,' thought Iván; 'but still I will go round,' and Iván went stealthily along by the shed. Iván stepped so softly in his bark shoes that he did not hear his own footsteps. As he reached the far corner, something seemed to flare up for a moment near the plough and to vanish again. Iván felt as if struck to the heart; and he stopped. Hardly had he stopped, when something flared up more brightly in the same place, and he clearly saw a man with a cap on his head, crouching down, with his back towards him, lighting a bunch of straw he held in his hand. Iván's heart fluttered within him like a bird. Straining every nerve, he approached with great strides, hardly feeling his legs under him. 'Ah,' thought Iván, 'now he won't escape! I'll catch him in the act!'

Iván was still some distance off, when suddenly he saw a bright light, but not in the same place as before, and not a small flame. The thatch had flared up at the eaves, the flames were reaching up to the roof, and, standing beneath it, Gabriel's whole figure was clearly visible.

Like a hawk swooping down on a lark, Iván rushed at Limping Gabriel. 'Now I'll have him; he shan't escape me!' thought Iván. But Gabriel must have heard his steps, and (however he managed it) glancing round, he scuttled away past the barn like a hare.

'You shan't escape!' shouted Iván, darting after him.

Just as he was going to seize Gabriel, the latter dodged him; but Iván managed to catch the skirt of Gabriel's coat. It tore right off, and Iván fell down. He recovered his feet, and shouting, 'Help! Seize him! Thieves! Murder!' ran on again. But meanwhile Gabriel had reached his own gate. There Iván overtook him and was about to seize him, when something struck Iván a stunning blow, as though a stone had hit his temple, quite deafening him. It was Gabriel who, seizing an oak wedge that lay near the gate, had struck out with all his might.

Iván was stunned; sparks flew before his eyes, then all grew dark and he staggered. When he came to his senses Gabriel was no longer there: it was as light as day, and from the side where his homestead was something roared and crackled like an engine at work. Iván turned round and saw that his back shed was all ablaze, and the side shed had also caught fire, and flames and smoke and bits of burning straw mixed with the smoke, were being driven towards his hut.

'What is this, friends?...' cried Iván, lifting his arms and striking his thighs. 'Why, all I had to do was just to snatch it out from under the eaves and trample on it! What is this, friends?...' he kept repeating. He wished to shout, but his breath failed him; his voice was gone. He wanted to run, but his legs would not obey him, and got in each other's way. He moved slowly, but again staggered and again his breath failed. He stood still till he had regained breath, and then went on. Before he had got round the back shed to reach the fire, the side shed was also all ablaze; and the corner of the hut and the covered gateway had caught fire as well. The flames were leaping out of the hut, and it was impossible to get into the yard. A large crowd had collected, but nothing could be done. The neighbours were carrying their belongings out of their own houses, and driving the cattle out of their own sheds. After Ivan's house, Gabriel's also caught fire, then, the wind rising, the flames spread to the other side of the street and half the village was burnt down.

At Ivan's house they barely managed to save his old father; and the family escaped in what they had on; everything else, except the horses that had been driven out to pasture for the night, was lost; all the cattle, the fowls on their perches, the carts, ploughs, and harrows, the women's trunks with their clothes, and the grain in the granaries—all were burnt up!

At Gabriel's, the cattle were driven out, and a few things saved from his house.

The fire lasted all night. Iván stood in front of his homestead and kept repeating, 'What is this?...Friends!...One need only have pulled it out and trampled on it!' But when the roof fell in, Iván rushed into the burning place, and seizing a charred beam, tried to drag it out. The women saw him, and called him back; but he pulled out the beam, and was going in again for another when he lost his footing and fell among the flames. Then his son made his way in after him and dragged him out. Iván had singed his hair and beard and burnt his clothes and scorched his hands, but he felt nothing. 'His grief has stupefied him,' said the people. The fire was burning itself out, but Iván still stood repeating: 'Friends!...What is this?...One need only have pulled it out!'

In the morning the village Elder's son came to fetch Iván.

'Daddy Iván, your father is dying! He has sent for you to say goodbye.'

Iván had forgotten about his father, and did not understand what was being said to him.

'What father?' he said. 'Whom has he sent for?'

'He sent for you, to say good-bye; he is dying in our cottage!

Come along, daddy Iván,' said the Elder's son, pulling him by the arm; and Iván followed the lad.

When he was being carried out of the hut, some burning straw had fallen on to the old man and burnt him, and he had been taken to the village Elder's in the farther part of the village, which the fire did not reach.

When Iván came to his father, there was only the Elder's wife in the hut, besides some little children on the top of the oven. All the rest were still at the fire. The old man, who was lying on a bench holding a wax candle (Wax candles are much used in the services of the Russian Church, and it is usual to place one in the hand of a dying man, especially when he receives unction) in his hand, kept turning his eyes towards the door. When his son entered, he moved a little. The old woman went up to him and told him that his son had come. He asked to have him brought nearer. Iván came closer.

'What did I tell you, Iván?' began the old man 'Who has burnt down the village?'

'It was he, father!' Iván answered. 'I caught him in the act. I saw him shove the firebrand into the thatch. I might have pulled away the burning straw and stamped it out, and then nothing would have happened.'

'Iván,' said the old man, 'I am dying, and you in your turn will have to face death. Whose is the sin?'

Iván gazed at his father in silence, unable to utter a word.

'Now, before God, say whose is the sin? What did I tell you?'

Only then Iván came to his senses and understood it all. He sniffed and said, 'Mine, father!' And he fell on his knees before his father, saying, 'Forgive me, father; I am guilty before you and before God.'

The old man moved his hands, changed the candle from his right hand to his left, and tried to lift his right hand to his forehead to cross himself, but could not do it, and stopped.

'Praise the Lord! Praise the Lord!' said he, and again he turned his eyes towards his son.

'Iván! I say, Iván!'

'What, father?'

'What must you do now?'

Iván was weeping.

'I don't know how we are to live now, father!' he said.

The old man closed his eyes, moved his lips as if to gather strength, and opening his eyes again, said: 'You'll manage. If you obey God's will, you'll manage!' He paused, then smiled, and said: 'Mind, Iván! Don't tell who started the fire! Hide another man's sin, and God will forgive two of yours!' And the old man took the candle in both hands and, folding them on his breast, sighed, stretched out, and died.

Iván did not say anything against Gabriel, and no one knew what had caused the fire.

And Ivan's anger against Gabriel passed away, and Gabriel wondered that Iván did not tell anybody. At first Gabriel felt afraid, but after awhile he got used to it. The men left off quarrelling, and then their families left off also. While rebuilding their huts, both families lived in one house; and when the village was rebuilt and they might have moved farther apart, Iván and Gabriel built next to each other, and remained neighbours as before.

They lived as good neighbours should. Iván Stcherbakóf remembered his old father's command to obey God's law, and quench a fire at the first spark; and if any one does him an injury he now tries not to revenge himself, but rather to set matters right again; and if any one gives him a bad word, instead of giving a worse in return, he tries to teach the other not to use evil words; and so he teaches his womenfolk and children. And Iván Stcherbakóf has got on his feet again, and now lives better even than he did before.

8

LUCERNE

July 20, 1857.
Yesterday evening I arrived at Lucerne, and put up at the best inn there, the Schweitzerhof. 'Lucerne, the chief city of the canton, situated on the shore of the Vierwaldstatter See,' says Murray, 'is one of the most romantic places of Switzerland: here cross three important highways, and it is only an hour's distance by steamboat to Mount Righi, from which is obtained one of the most magnificent views in the world.'

Whether that be true or no, other guides say the same thing, and consequently at Lucerne there are throngs of travellers of all nationalities, especially the English.

The magnificent five-storied building of the Hotel Schweitzerhof is situated on the quay, at the very edge of the lake, where in olden times there used to be the crooked covered wooden bridge with chapels on the corners and pictures on the roof. Now, thanks to the tremendous inroad of Englishmen, with their necessities, their tastes, and their money, they have torn down the old bridge, and in its place erected a granite quay, straight as a stick. On the quay they have built straight, quadrangular five-storied houses; in front of the houses they have set out two rows of lindens and provided them with supports, and between the lindens is the usual supply of green benches.

This is the promenade; and here back and forth stroll the Englishwomen in their Swiss straw hats, and the Englishmen in simple and comfortable attire, and rejoice in their work. Possibly these quays and houses and lindens and Englishmen would be excellent in their way anywhere else, but here they seem discordant amid this strangely magnificent, and at the same time indescribably harmonious and smiling nature.

As soon as I went up to my room, and opened the window facing the lake, the beauty of the sheet of water, of the mountains, and of the sky, at the first moment literally dazzled and overwhelmed me. I experienced an inward unrest, and the necessity of expressing in some manner the feelings that suddenly filled my soul to overflowing. I felt a desire to embrace, powerfully to embrace, someone, to tickle him, or to pinch him; in short to do to him and to myself something extraordinary.

It was seven o'clock in the evening. The rain had been falling all day, but now it had cleared.

The lake, iridescent as melted sulphur, and dotted with boats, which left behind them vanishing trails, spread out before my windows smooth, motionless as it were, between the variegated green shores. Farther away it was contracted between two monstrous headlands, and, darkling, set itself against and disappeared behind a confused pile of mountains, clouds, and glaciers. In the foreground stretched a panorama of moist, fresh green shores, with reeds, meadows, gardens, and villas. Farther away, the dark green wooded heights, crowned with the ruins of feudal castles; in the background, the rolling, pale lilac-coloured vista of mountains, with fantastic peaks built up of crags and pallid snow-capped summits. And everything was bathed in a fresh, transparent azure atmosphere, and kindled by the warm rays of the setting sun, bursting forth through the riven skies.

Not on the lake or on the mountains or in the skies was there a single completed line, a single unmixed colour, a single moment of repose; everywhere motion, irregularity, fantasy, endless conglomeration and variety of shades and lines; and above all, a calm, a softness, a unity, and the inevitability of beauty.

And here amid this indeterminate, kaleidoscopic, unfettered loveliness, before my very window, stretched stupidly, compelling the gaze, the white line of the quay, the lindens with their supports, and the green seats, miserable, tasteless creations of human ingenuity, not subordinated, like the distant villas and ruins, to the general harmony of the beautiful scene, but on the contrary brutally opposed to it...

Constantly, though against my will, my eyes were attracted to that horribly straight line of the quay; and mentally I should have liked to get rid of it, to demolish it like a black spot which should disfigure the nose beneath one's eye.

But the quay with the sauntering Englishmen remained where it was, and I involuntarily tried to find a point of view where it would be out of my sight. I succeeded in finding such a view; and till dinner was ready I took delight, alone by myself in this incomplete and therefore the more enjoyable feeling of oppression that one experiences in the solitary contemplation of natural beauty.

About half past seven I was called to dinner. Two long tables, accommodating at least a hundred persons, were spread in the great, magnificently-decorated dining room on the first floor. The silent gathering of the guests lasted three minutes, the rustle of women's gowns, the soft steps, the softly spoken words addressed to the courtly and elegant waiters. And all the places were occupied by ladies and gentlemen dressed elegantly, even richly, and for the most part in perfect taste.

As is apt to be the case in Switzerland, the majority of the guests were English, and this gave the ruling characteristics of the common table: that is, a strict decorum regarded as an obligation, a reserve founded not in pride but in the absence of any necessity for social relationship, and finally a uniform sense of satisfaction felt by each in the comfortable and agreeable gratification of his wants.

On all sides gleamed the whitest laces, the whitest collars, the whitest teeth, natural and artificial, the whitest complexions and hands. But the faces, many of which were very handsome, bore the expression merely of individual prosperity, and absolute absence of interest in all that surrounded them unless it bore directly on their own individual selves; and the white hands, glittering with rings or protected by mitts, moved only for the purpose of straightening collars, cutting meat, or filling wine-glasses; no soul-felt emotion was betrayed in these actions.

Occasionally members of some one family would exchange remarks in subdued voices, about the excellence of such and such a dish or wine, or about the beauty of the view from Mount Righi.

Individual tourists, whether men or women, sat beside one another in silence, and did not even seem to see one another. If it happened occasionally that, out of this five-score human beings, two spoke to each other, the topic of their conversation was certain to be the weather, or the ascent of the Righi.

Knives and forks scarcely rattled on the plates, so perfect was the observance of propriety; and no one dared to convey peas and vegetables to the mouth otherwise than on the fork. The waiters, involuntarily subdued by the universal silence, asked in a whisper what wine you would be pleased to order.

Such dinners always depress me: I dislike them, and before they are over I become blue. It always seems to me as if I had done something wrong; just as when I was a boy I was set upon a chair in consequence of some naughtiness and bidden ironically, 'Now rest a little while, my dear young fellow.' And all the time my young blood was pulsing through my veins, and in the other room I could hear the merry shouts of my brothers.

I used to try to rebel against this feeling of being choked

down, which I experienced at such dinners, but in vain. All these dead-and-alive faces have an irresistible influence over me, and I myself become also as one dead. I have no desires, I have no thoughts; I do not even observe.

At first I attempted to enter into conversation with my neighbours; but I got no response beyond the phrases which had probably been repeated in that place a hundred thousand times, a hundred thousand times by the same persons.

And yet these people were by no means all stupid and feelingless; but evidently many of them, though they seemed so dead, led self-centred lives, just as I did, and in many cases far more complicated and interesting ones than my own. Why, then, should they deprive themselves of one of the greatest enjoyments of life, the enjoyment that comes from the intercourse of man with man?

How different it used to be in our pension at Paris, where twenty of us, belonging to as many different nationalities, professions, and individualities, met together at a common table, and, under the influence of the Gallic sociability, found the keenest zest!

There, immediately, from one end of the table to the other, the conversation, sandwiched with witticisms and puns, though often in a broken speech, became general. There everyone, without being solicitous for the proprieties, said whatever came into his head. There we had our own philosopher, our own disputant, our own bel esprit, our own butt—all common property.

There, immediately after dinner, we would move the table to one side, and, without paying too much attention to rhythm, take to dancing the polka on the dusty carpet, and often keep it up till evening. There, though we were rather flirtatious, and not overwise or dignified, still we were human beings.

And the Spanish countess with romantic proclivities, and the Italian abbate, who insisted on declaiming from the 'Divine Comedy' after dinner, and the American doctor who had the entrée into the Tuileries, and the young dramatic author with his long hair, and the pianist who, according to her own account, had composed the best polka in existence, and the unhappy widow who was a beauty, and wore three rings on every finger—all of us enjoyed this society, which, though somewhat superficial, was human and pleasant. And we each carried away from it hearty recollections of the others, superficial or serious, as the case might be.

But at these English table-d'hote dinners, as I look at all these laces, ribbons, jewels, pomaded locks, and silken gowns, I often think how many living women would be happy, and would make others happy, with these adornments.

Strange to think how many friends and lovers—most fortunate friends and lovers—are, perhaps, sitting side by side without knowing it! And God knows why they never come to this knowledge, and never give each other this happiness, which they might so easily give, and which they so long for.

I began to feel depressed, as usual, after such a dinner; and, without waiting for dessert, I sallied out in the most gloomy frame of mind for a constitutional through the city. My melancholy frame of mind was not relieved, but was rather confirmed, by the narrow, muddy streets without lanterns, the shuttered shops, the encounters with drunken workmen, and with women hastening after water, or in bonnets, glancing around them as they glided down the alleys or along the walls.

It was perfectly dark in the streets when I returned to the hotel without casting a glance about me, or having an idea in my head. I hoped that sleep would put an end to my melancholy. I experienced that horrible spiritual chill, loneliness, and heaviness, which sometimes, without any reason, beset those who are just arrived in any new place.

Looking down at my feet, I walked along the quay to the Schweitzerhof, when suddenly my ear was struck by the strains of a peculiar but thoroughly agreeable and sweet music.

These strains had an immediately enlivening effect on me. It was as if a bright, cheerful light had poured into my soul. I felt contented, gay. My slumbering attention was awakened again to all surrounding objects; and the beauty of the night and the lake, to which, till then, I had been indifferent, suddenly came over me with quickening force like something new.

I involuntarily took in at a glance the dark sky with grey clouds flecking its deep blue, now lighted by the rising moon, the glassy, dark green lake, with its surface reflecting the lighted windows, and far away the snowy mountains; and I heard the croaking of the frogs over on the Froschenburg shore, and the dewy fresh call of the quail.

Directly in front of me, in the spot whence the sounds of music had first come, and which still especially attracted my attention, I saw, amid the semi-darkness on the street, a throng of people standing in a semicircle, and in front of the crowd, at a little distance, a small man in dark clothes.

Behind the throng and the man, there stood out harmoniously against the blue, ragged sky, grey and blue, the black tops of a few Lombardy poplars in some garden, and, rising majestically on high, the two stern spires that stand on the towers of the ancient cathedral.

I drew nearer, and the strains became more distinct. At some distance I could clearly distinguish the full accords of a guitar, sweetly swelling in the evening air, and several voices, which, while taking turns with one another, did not sing any definite theme, but gave suggestions of one in places wherever the melody was most pronounced.

The theme was in somewhat the nature of a mazurka, sweet and graceful. The voices sounded now near at hand, now far distant; now a bass was heard, now a tenor, now a falsetto such as the Tyrolese warblers are wont to sing.

It was not a song, but the graceful, masterly sketch of a song. I could not comprehend what it was, but it was beautiful.

Those voluptuous, soft chords of the guitar, that sweet, gentle melody, that solitary figure of the man in black, amid the fantastic environment of the dark lake, the gleaming moon, and the twin spires of the cathedral rising in majestic silence, and the black tops of the poplars—all was strange and perfectly beautiful, or at least seemed so to me.

All the confused, arbitrary impressions of life suddenly became full of meaning and beauty. It seemed to me as if a fresh fragrant flower had sprung up in my soul. In place of the weariness, dullness, and indifference toward everything in the world, which I had been feeling the moment before, I experienced a necessity for love, a fullness of hope, and an unbounded enjoyment of life.

'What does thou desire, what doest thou long for?' an inner voice seemed to say. 'Here it is. Thou art surrounded on all sides by beauty and poetry. Breathe it in, in full, deep draughts, as long as thou hast strength. Enjoy it to the full extent of thy capacity 'T is all thine, all blessed!'....

I drew nearer. The little man was, as it seemed, a travelling Tyrolese. He stood before the windows of the hotel, one leg advanced, his head thrown back; and, as he thrummed on the guitar, he sang his graceful song in all those different voices.

I immediately felt an affection for this man, and a gratefulness for the change which he had brought about in me.

The singer, as far as I was able to judge, was dressed in an old black coat. He had short black hair, and he wore a civilian's hat which was no longer new. There was nothing artistic in his attire, but his clever and youthfully gay motions and pose, together with his diminutive stature, formed a pleasing and at the same time pathetic spectacle.

On the steps, in the windows, and on the balconies of the brilliantly lighted hotel, stood ladies handsomely decorated and attired, gentlemen with polished collars, porters and lackeys in gold-embroidered liveries; in the street, in the semicircle of the crowd, and farther along on the sidewalk, among the lindens, were gathered groups of well-dressed waiters, cooks in white caps and aprons, and young girls wandering about with arms about each others' waists.

All, it seemed, were under the influence of the same feeling as I myself experienced. All stood in silence around the singer, and listened attentively. Silence reigned, except in the pauses of the song, when there came from far away across the waters the regular click of a hammer, and from the Froschenburg shore rang in fascinating, monotone the voices of the frogs, interrupted by the mellow, monotonous call of the quail.

The little man in the darkness, in the midst of the street, poured out his heart like a nighingale, in couplet after couplet, song after song. Though I had come close to him, his singing continued to give me greater and greater gratification.

His voice, which was of great power, was extremely pleasant and tender; the taste and feeling for rhythm which he displayed in the control of it were extraordinary, and proved that he had great natural gifts.

After he sung each couplet, he invariably repeated the theme in variation, and it was evident that all his graceful variations came to him at the instant, spontaneously.

Among the crowd, and above on the Schweitzerhof, and near by on the boulevard, were heard frequent murmurs of approval, though generally the most respectful silence reigned.

The balconies and the windows kept filling more and more with handsomely-dressed men and women leaning on their elbows, and picturesquely illuminated by the lights in the house.

Promenaders came to a halt, and in the darkness on the quay stood men and women in little groups. Near me, at some distance from the common crowd, stood an aristocratic cook and lackey, smoking their cigars.

The cook was forcibly impressed by the music, and at every high falsetto note enthusiastically nodded his head to the lackey, and nudged him with his elbow with an expression of astonishment which seemed to say, 'How he sings! hey?'

The lackey, by whose undissimulated smile I could mark the depth of feeling he experienced, replied to the cook's nudges by shrugging his shoulders, as if to show that it was hard enough for him to be made enthusiastic, and that he had heard much better music.

In one of the pauses of his song, while the minstrel was clearing his throat, I asked the lackey who he was, and if he often came there.

'Twice in the summer he comes here,' replied the lackey. 'He is from Aargau; he gets his livelihood by begging.'

'Tell me, do many like him come round here?' I asked.

'Oh, yes,' replied the lackey, not comprehending the full force of what I asked; but immediately after, recollecting himself, he added, 'Oh, no. This one is the only one I ever heard here. No one else.'

At this moment the little man had finished his first song, was briskly twanging his guitar, and said something in his German patois, which I could not understand, but which brought forth a hearty round of laughter from the surrounding throng.

'What was that he said?' I asked.

'He said his throat is dried up, he would like some wine,' replied the lackey, who was standing near me.

'What? is he rather fond of the glass?'

'Yes, all that sort of people are,' replied the lackey, smiling and pointing at the minstrel.

The minstrel took off his cap, and swinging his guitar went toward the hotel. Raising his head, he addressed the ladies and gentlemen standing by the windows and on the balconies, saying in a half-Italian, half-German accent, and with the same intonation as jugglers use in speaking to their audiences:—

'Messieurs et mesdames, si vous croyez que je gagne quelque chose, vous vous trompez: je ne suis qu'un pauvre tiaple.'

He stood in silence a moment, but as no one gave him anything, he once more took up his guitar, and said:

'A présent, messieurs et mesdames, je vous chanterai l'air du Righi.'

His hotel audience made no response, but stood in expectation of the coming song. Below on the street a laugh went round, probably in part because he had expressed himself so strangely, and in part because no one had given him anything.

I gave him a few centimes, which he deftly changed from one hand to the other, and bestowed them in his vest-pocket; and then, replacing his cap, began once more to sing; it was the graceful, sweet Tyrolese melody which he had called 'l'air du Righi'.

This song, which formed the last on his programme, was even better than the preceding, and from all sides in the wondering throng were heard sounds of approbation.

He finished. Again he swung his guitar, took off his cap, held it out in front of him, went two or three steps nearer to the windows, and again repeated his stock phrase: 'Messieurs et mesdames, si vous croyez que je gagne quelque chose,' which he evidently considered to be very shrewd and witty; but in his voice and motions I perceived now a certain irresolution and childish timidity which were especially touching in a person of such diminutive stature.

This elegant public, still picturesquely grouped in the lighted windows and on the balconies, were shining in their rich attire; a few conversed in soberly discreet tones, apparently about the singer who was standing there below them with outstretched hand; others gazed down with attentive curiosity on the little black figure; on one balcony could be heard a young girl's merry, ringing laughter.

In the crowd below the talk and laughter kept growing louder and louder.

The singer for the third time repeated his phrase, but in a still weaker voice, and did not even end the sentence; and again he stretched his hand with his cap, but instantly drew it back. Again, not one of those brilliantly dressed scores of people standing to listen to him threw him a penny.

The crowd laughed heartlessly.

The little singer, so it seemed to me, shrunk more into himself, took his guitar into his other hand, lifted his cap, and said:

'Messieurs et mesdames, je vous remercie, et je vous souhais une bonne nuit.'

Then he put on his hat.

The crowd cackled with laughter and satisfaction. The handsome ladies and gentlemen, clamly exchanging remarks, withdrew gradually from the balconies. On the boulevard the promenading began once more. The street, which had been still during the singing, assumed its wonted liveliness; a few men, however, stood at some distance, and, without approaching the singer, looked at him and laughed.

I heard the little man muttering something between his teeth, as he turned away; and I saw him, apparently growing more and more diminutive, start toward the city with brisk steps. The promenaders, who had been looking at him, followed him at some distance, still making merry at his expense...

My mind was in a whirl; I could not comprehend what it all meant; and still standing in the same place, I gazed abstractedly into the darkness after the little man, who was fast disappearing, as he went with ever increasing swiftness with long strides into the city, followed by the merrymaking promenaders.

I was overmastered by a feeling of pain, of bitterness, and, above all, of shame for the little man, for the crowd, for myself, as if it were I who had asked for money and received none; as if it were I who had been turned to ridicule.

Without looking any longer, feeling my heart oppressed, I also hurried with long strides toward the entrance of the Schweitzerhof. I could not explain the feeling that overmastered me; only there was something like a stone, from which I could not free myself, weighing down my soul and oppressing me.

At the stately, well-lighted entrance I met the Swiss, who politely made way for me. An English family was also at the door. A portly, handsome, tall gentleman, with black side-whiskers, in a black hat, and with a plaid on one arm, while in his hand he carried a costly cane, came out slowly, and full of importance. Leaning on his arm was a lady, who wore a raw silk gown and a bonnet with bright ribbons and the most charming laces. With them was a pretty, fresh-looking young lady, in a graceful Swiss hat, with a feather, 'à la mousquetaire'; from under it escaped long, light yellow curls, softly encircling her fair face. In front of them skipped a buxom girl of ten, with round, white knees which showed from under her thin embroideries. 'What a lovely night!' the lady was saying in a sweet, happy voice, as I passed them.

'Oh, yes,' growled the Englishman, lazily; and it was evident that he found it so enjoyable to be alive in the world, that it was too much trouble even to speak.

And it seemed as if all of them alike found it so comfortable and easy, so light and free, to be alive in the world, their faces and motions expressed such perfect indifference to the lives of everyone else, and such absolute confidence, that it was to them that the Swiss made way, and bowed so profoundly, and that when they returned they would find clean, comfortable beds and rooms, and that all this was bound to be, and was their indefeasible right, that I could not help contrasting them with the wandering minstrel, who, weary, perhaps hungry, full of shame, was retreating before the laughing crowd. And then, suddenly, I comprehended what it was that oppressed my heart with such a load of heaviness, and I felt an indescribable anger against these people.

Twice I walked up and down past the Englishman, and each time, without turning out for him, my elbow punched him, which gave me a feeling of indescribable satisfaction; and then, darting down the steps, I hastened through the darkness in the direction taken by the little man on his way to the city.

Overtaking three men, walking together, I asked them where the singer was; they laughed, and pointed straight ahead. There he was, walking alone with brisk steps; no one was with him; all the time, as it seemed to me, he was indulging in bitter monologue.

I caught up with him, and proposed to him to go somewhere with me and drink a bottle of wine. He kept on with his rapid walk, and looked at me indignantly; but when it dawned on him what I meant, he halted.

'Well, I will not refuse, if you are so kind,' said he; 'here is a little café, we can go in there. It's very ordinary,' he added, pointing to a drinking-salon that was still open.

His expression 'very ordinary' involuntarily suggested to my mind the idea of not going to a very ordinary café, but to go to the Schweitzerhof, where those who had been listening to him were. Notwithstanding the fact that several times he showed a sort of timid disquietude at the idea of going to the Schweitzerhof, declaring that it was too fashionable for him there, still I insisted on carrying out my purpose; and he, already pretending that he was not in the least abashed, and gayly swinging his guitar, went back with me across the quay.

A few loiterers who had happened along as I was talking with the minstrel, and had stopped to hear what I had to say, now, after arguing among themselves, followed us to the very entrance of the hotel, evidently expecting from the Tyrolese some further demonstration.

I ordered a bottle of wine of a waiter whom I met in the hall. The waiter smiled and looked at us, and went by without answering. The head waiter, to whom I addressed myself with the same order, listened to me and, measuring the minstrel's modest little figure from head to foot, sternly ordered the waiter to take us to the room at the left.

The room at the left was a bar-room for simple people. In the corner of this room a hunchbacked maid was washing dishes. The whole furniture consisted of bare wooden tables and benches.

The waiter who came to serve us looked at us with a supercilious smile, thrust his hands in his pockets, and exchanged some remarks with the humpbacked dishwasher. He evidently tried to give us to understand that he felt himself immeasurably higher than the minstrel, both in dignity and social position, so that he considered it not only an indignity, but actually ridiculous, that he was called on to serve us.

'Do you wish vin ordinaire?' he asked, with a knowing look, winking toward my companion and switching his napkin from one hand to the other.

'Champagne, and your very best,' said I, endeavouring to assume my haughtiest and most imposing appearance.

But neither my champagne, nor my endeavour to look haughty and imposing, had the least effect on the servant; he smiled incredulously, loitered a moment or two gazing at us, took time enough to glance at his gold watch, and with leisurely steps, as if going out for a walk, left the room.

Soon he returned with the wine, bringing two other waiters with him. These two sat down near the dishwasher, and gazed at us with amused attention and a bland smile, just as parents gaze at their children when they are gently playing. Only the humpbacked dishwasher, it seemed to me, did not look at us scornfully but sympathetically.

Though it was trying and awkward to lunch with the minstrel, and to play the entertainer, under the fire of all these waiters' eyes, I tried to do my duty with as little constraint as possible.

In the lighted room I could see him better. He was a small but symmetrically built and muscular man, though almost a dwarf in stature; he had bristly black hair, teary big black eyes, bushy eyebrows, and a thoroughly pleasant, attractively shaped mouth. He had little side-whiskers, his hair was short, his attire was very simple and mean. He was not over-clean, was ragged and sunburnt, and in general had the look of a labouring-man. He was far more like a poor tradesman than an artist.

Only in his ever humid and brilliant eyes, and in his firm mouth, was there any sign of originality or genius. By his face it might be conjectured that his age was between twenty-five and forty; in reality, he was thirty-seven.

Here is what he related to me, with good-natured readiness and evident sincerity, of his life. He was a native of Aargau. In early childhood he had lost his father and mother; other relatives he had none. He had never owned any property. He had been apprenticed to a carpenter; but twenty-two years previously one of his arms had been attacked by caries, which had prevented him from ever working again.

From childhood he had been fond of singing, and he began to be a singer. Occasionally strangers had given him money. With this he had learned his profession, bought his guitar, and now for eighteen years he had been wandering about through Switzerland and Italy, singing before hotels. His whole luggage consisted of his guitar, and a little purse in which, at the present time, there was only a franc and a half. That would have to suffice for supper and lodgings this night.

Every year now for eighteen years he had made the round of the best and most popular resorts of Switzerland—Zurich, Lucerne, Interlaken, Chamounix, etc.; by the way of the St. Bernard he would go down into Italy, and return over the St. Gotthard, or through Savoy. Just at present it was rather hard for him to walk, as he had caught a cold, causing him to suffer from some trouble in his legs—he called it Gliederzucht, or rheumatism—which grew more severe from year to yyear; and, moreover, his voice and eyes had grown weaker. Nevertheless, he was on his way to Interlaken, Aix-les-Bains, and thence over the little St. Bernard to Italy, which he was very fond of. It was evident that on the whole he was well content with his life.

When I asked him why he returned home, if he had any relatives there, or a house and land, his mouth parted in a gay smile, and he replied, '*Oui, le sucre est bon, il est doux pour les enfants*!' and he winked at the servants.

I did not catch his meaning, but the group of servants burst out laughing.

'No, I have nothing of the sort, but still I should always want to go back,' he explained to me. 'I go home because there is always a something that draws one to one's native place.'

And once more he repeated with a shrewd, self-satisfied smile, his phrase, '*Oui, le sucre est bon*,' and then laughed good-naturedly.

The servants were very much amused, and laughed heartily; only the hunchbacked dishwasher looked earnestly from her big kindly eyes at the little man, and picked up his cap for him, when, as we talked, he once knocked it off the bench. I have noticed that wandering minstrels, acrobats, even jugglers, delight in calling themselves artists, and several times I hinted to my comrade that he was an artist; but he did not at all accept this designation, but with perfect simplicity looked on his work as a means of existence.

When I asked him if he had not himself written the songs which he sang, he showed great surprise at such a strange question, and replied that the words of whatever he sang were all of old Tyrolese origin.

'But how about that song of the Righi? I think that cannot be very ancient,' I suggested.

'Oh, that was composed about fifteen years ago. There was a

German in Basle; he was a clever man; it was he who composed it. A splendid song. You see he composed it especially for travellers.'

And he began to repeat the words of the Righi song, which he liked so well, translated them into French as he went along.

'If you wish to go to Righi,
You will not need shoes to Wegis
(For you go that far by steamboat),
But from Wegis take a stout staff,
Also on your arm a maiden;
Drink a glass of wine on starting,
Only do not drink too freely,
For if you desire to drink here,
You must earn the right to, first.'

'Oh! a splendid song!' he exclaimed, as he finished. The servants, evidently, also found the song much to their mind, because they came up closer to us.

'Yes, but who was it composed the music?' I asked.

'Oh, no one at all; you know you must have something new when you are going to sing for strangers.'

When the ice was brought, and I had given my comrade a glass of champagne, he seemed somewhat ill at ease, and, glancing at the servants, he turned and twisted on the bench.

We touched our glasses to the health of all artists; he drank half a glass, then he seemed to be collecting his ideas, and knit his brows in deep thought.

'It is long since I have tasted such wine, je ne vous dis que ça. In Italy the vino d'Asti is excellent, but this is still better. Ah! Italy; it is splendid to be there!' he added.

'Yes, there they know how to appreciate music and artists,' said I, trying to bring him round to the evening's mischance before the Schweitzerhof.

'No,' he replied. 'There, as far as music is concerned, I cannot give anybody satisfaction. The Italians are themselves musicians, none like them in the world; but I know only Tyrolese songs. They are something of a novelty to them, though.'

'Well, you find rather more generous gentlemen there, don't you?' I went on to say, anxious to make him share in my resentment against the guests of the Schweitzerhof. 'There it would not be possible to find a big hotel frequented by rich people, where, out of a hundred listening to an artist's singing, not one would give him anything.'

My question utterly failed of the effect that I expected. It did not enter his head to be indignant with them; on the contrary, he saw in my remark an implied slur on his talent which had failed of its reward, and he hastened to set himself right before me. 'It is not every time that you get anything,' he remarked; 'sometimes one isn't in good voice, or you are tired; now today I have been walking ten hours, and singing almost all the time. That is hard. And these important aristocrats do not always care to listen to Tyrolese songs.'

'But still, how can they help giving?' I insisted. He did not comprehend my remark.

'That's nothing,' he said; 'but here the principal thing is, on est tres serré pour la police that's what's the trouble. Here, according to these republican laws, you are not allowed to sing; but in Italy you can go wherever you please, no one says a word. Here, if they want to let you, they let you; but if they don't want to, then they can throw you into jail.'

'What? That's incredible!'

'Yes, it is true. If you have been wanted once, and are found singing again, they may put you in jail. I was kept there three months once,' he said, smiling as if that were one of his pleasantest recollections.

'Oh! that is terrible!' I exclaimed. 'What was the reason?'

'That was in consequence of one of the new laws of the republic,' he went on to explain, growing animated. 'They cannot comprehend here that a poor fellow must earn his living somehow. If I were not a cripple, I would work. But what harm do I do to any one in the world by my singing? What does it mean? The rich can live as they wish, but like myself can't live at all. What does it mean by laws of the republic? If that is the way they run, then we don't want a republic. Isn't that so, my dear sir? We don't want a republic, but we want…we simply want…we want'…he hesitated a little,…'we want natural laws.'

I filled up his glass.

'You are not drinking,' I said.

He took the glass in his hand, and bowed to me.

'I know what you wish,' he said, blinking his eyes at me, and threatening me with his finger. 'You wish to make me drunk, so as to see what you can get out of me; but no, you shan't have that gratification.'

'Why should I make you drunk?' I inquired. 'All I wished was to give you a pleasure.'

He seemed really sorry that he had offended me by interpreting my insistence so harshly. He grew confused, stood up, and touched my elbow.

'No, no,' said he, looking at me with a beseeching expression in his moist eyes. 'I was only joking.'

And immediately after he made use of some horribly uncultivated slang expression, intended to signify that I was, nevertheless, a fine young man.

In this fashion the minstrel and I continued to drink and converse; and the waiters continued to stare at us unceremoniously, and, as it seemed, to ridicule us.

In spite of the interest which our conversation aroused in me, I could not avoid taking notice of their behaviour; and I confess I began to grow more and more angry.

One of the waiters arose, came up to the little man, and, looking at the top of his head, began to smile. I was already full of wrath against the inmates of the hotel, and had not yet had a chance to pour it out on any one; and now I confess I was in the highest degree irritated by this audience of waiters.

The Swiss, not removing his hat, came into the room, and sat down near me, leaning his elbows on the table. This last circumstance, which was so insulting to my dignity or my vainglory, completely enraged me, and gave an outlet for all the wrath which the whole evening long had been boiling within me. Why had he so humbly bowed when he had met me before, and now, because I was sitting with the travelling minstrel, did he come and take his place near me so rudely? I was entirely overmastered by that boiling, angry indignation which I enjoy in myself, which I sometimes endeavour to stimulate when it comes over me, because it has an exhilarating effect on me, and gives me, if only for a short time, a certain extraordinary flexibility, energy, and strength in all my physical and moral faculties.

I leaped to my feet.

'Whom are you laughing at?' I screamed at the waiter; and I felt my face turn pale, and my lips involuntarily set together.

'I am not laughing, I only…' replied the waiter, moving away from me.

'Yes, you are; you are laughing at this gentleman. And what right have you to come, and to take a seat here, when there are guests? Don't you dare to sit down!' The Swiss, muttering something, got up and turned to the door.

'What right have you to make sport of this gentleman, and to sit down by him, when he is a guest, and you are a waiter? Why didn't you laugh at me this evening at dinner, and come and sit down beside me? Because he is meanly dressed, and sings in the streets? Is that the reason? and because I have better clothes? He is poor, but he is a thousand times better than you are; that I am sure of, because he has never insulted any one, but you have insulted him.'

'I didn't mean anything,' replied my enemy, the waiter. 'Did I disturb him by sitting down?'

The waiter did not understand me, and my German was wasted on him. The rude Swiss was about to take the waiter's part; but I fell upon him so impetuously that the Swiss pretended not to understand me, and waved his hand.

The hunchbacked dishwasher, either because she perceived my wrathful state, and feared a scandal, or possibly because she shared my views, took my part, and, trying to force her way between me and the porter, told him to hold his tongue, saying that I was right, but at the same time urging me to calm myself.

The minstrel's face presented a most pitiable, terrified expression; and evidently he did not understand why I was angry, and what I wanted; and he urged me to let him go away as soon as possible.

But the eloquence of wrath burned within me more and more. I understood it all, the throng that had made merry at his expense, and his audience who had not given him anything; and not for all the world would I have held my peace.

I believe that, if the waiters and the Swiss had not been so submissive, I should have taken delight in having a brush with them, or striking the defenseless English girl on the head with a stick. If at that moment I had been at Sevastopol, I should have taken delight in devoting myself to slaughtering and killing in the English trench.

'And why did you take this gentleman and me into this room, and not into the other? What?' I thundered at the swiss, seizing him by the arm so that he could not escape from me. 'What right had you to judge by his appearance that this gentleman must be served in this room, and not in that? Have not all guests who pay equal rights in hotels? Not only in a republic, but in all the world! Your scurvy republic!...Equality, indeed! You would not dare to take an Englishman into this room, not even those Englishmen who have heard this gentleman free of cost; that is, who have stolen from him, each one of them, the few centimes which ought to have been given to him. How did you dare to take us to this room?'

'That room is closed,' said the porter.

'No,' I cried, 'that isn't true; it isn't closed.'

'Then you know best.'

'I know...I know that you are lying.'

The Swiss turned his back on me.

'Eh! What is to be said?' he muttered.

'What is to be said?' I cried. 'Now conduct us instantly into that room!'

In spite of the dishwasher's warning, and the entreaties of the minstrel, who would have preferred to go home, I insisted on seeing the head waiter, and went with my guest into the big dining room. The head waiter, hearing my angry voice, and seeing my menacing face, avoided a quarrel, and, with contemptuous servility, said that I might go wherever I pleased. I could not prove to the Swiss that he had lied, because he had hastened out of sight before I went into the hall.

The dining room was, in fact, open and lighted; and at one of the tables sat an Englishman and a lady, eating their supper. Although we were shown to a special table, I took the dirty minstrel to the very one where the Englishman was, and bade the waiter bring to us there the unfinished bottle.

The two guests at first looked with surprised, then with angry, eyes at the little man, who, more dead than alive, was sitting near me. They talked together in a low tone; then the lady pushed back her plate, her silk dress rustled, and both of them left the room. Through the glass doors I saw the Englishman saying something in an angry voice to the waiter, and pointing with his hand in our direction. The waiter put his head through the door, and looked at us. I waited with pleasurable anticipation for some one to come and order us out, for then I could have found a full outlet for all my indignation. But fortunately, though at the time I felt injured, we were left in peace. The minstrel, who before had fought shy of the wine, now eagerly drank all that was left in the bottle, so that he might make his escape as quickly as possible.

He, however, expressed his gratitude with deep feeling, as it seemed to me, for his entertainment. His teary eyes grew still more humid and brilliant, and he made use of a most strange and complicated phrase of gratitude. But still very pleasant to me was the sentence in which he said that if everybody treated artists as I had been doing, it would be very good, and ended by wishing me all manner of happiness. We went out into the hall together. There stood the servants, and my enemy the Swiss apparently airing his grievances against me before them. All of them, I thought, looked at me as if I were a man who had lost his wits. I treated the little man exactly like an equal, before all that audience of servants; and then, with all the respect that I was able to express in my behaviour, I took off my hat, and pressed his hand with its dry and hardened fingers.

The servants pretended not to pay the slightest attention to me. Only one of them indulged in a sarcastic laugh. As soon as the minstrel had bowed himself out, and disappeared in the darkness, I went up-stairs to my room, intending to sleep off all these impressions and the foolish, childish anger which had come upon me so unexpectedly. But, finding that I was too much excited to sleep, I once more went down into the street with the intention of walking until I should have recovered my equanimity, and, I must confess, with the secret hope that I might accidentally come across the porter or the waiter or the Englishman, and show them all their rudeness, and, most of all, their unfairness. But beyond the Swiss, who when he saw me turned his back, I met no one; and I began to promenade in absolute solitude back and forth along the quay.

'This is an example of the strange fate of poetry,' said I to myself, having grown a little calmer. 'All love it, all are in search of it; it is the only thing in life that men love and seek, and yet no one recognizes its power, no one prizes this best treasure of the world, and those who give it to men are not rewarded. Ask any one you please, ask all these guests of the schweitzerhof, what is the most precious treasure in the world, and all, or ninety-nine out of a hundred, putting on a sardonic expression, will say that the best thing in the world is money.

'"Maybe, though, this does not please you, or coincide with your elevated ideas," it will be urged; "but what is to be done if human life is so constituted that money alone is capable of giving a man happiness? I cannot force my mind not to see the world as it is," it will be added, "that is, to see the truth."

'Pitiable is your intellect, pitiable the happiness which you desire! And you yourselves, unhappy creatures, not knowing what you desire,...why have you all left your fatherland, your relatives, your money-making trades and occupations, and come to this little Swiss city of Lucerne? Why did you all this evening gather on the balconies, and in respectful silence listen to the little beggar's song? And if he had been willing to sing longer, you would have been silent and listened longer. What! could money, even millions of it, have driven you all from your country, and brought you all together in this little nook of Lucerne? Could money have gathered you all on the balconies to stand for half an hour silent and motionless? No! One thing compels you to do it, and will forever have a stronger influence than all the other impulses of life: the longing for poetry which you know, which you do not realize, but feel, always will feel as long as you have any human sensibilities. The word "poetry" is a mockery to you; you make use of it as a sort of ridiculous reproach; you regard the love for poetry as something meant for children and silly girls, and you make sport of them for it. For yourselves you must have something more definite.

'But children look upon life in a healthy way; they recognize and love what man ought to love, and what gives happiness. But life has so deceived and perverted you, that you ridicule the only thing that you really love, and you seek for what you hate and for what gives you unhappiness.

'You are so perverted that you did not perceive what obligations you were under to the poor Tyrolese who rendered you a pure delight; but at the same time you feel needlessly obliged to humiliate yourselves before some lord, which gives you neither pleasure nor profit, but rather causes you to sacrifice your comfort and convenience. What absurdity! what incomprehensible lack of reason!

'But it was not this that made the most powerful impression on me this evening. This blindness to all that gives happiness, this unconsciousness of poetic enjoyment, I can almost comprehend, or at least I have become wonted to it, since I have almost everywhere met with it in the course of my life; the harsh, unconscious churlishness of the crowd was no novelty to me; whatever those who argue in favour of popular sentiment may say, the throng is a conglomeration of very possibly good people, but of people who touch each other only on their coarse animal sides, and express only the weakness and harshness of human nature. But how was it that you, children of a free, humane people, you Christians, you simply as human beings, repaid with coldness and ridicule the poor beggar who gave you a pure enjoyment? But no, in your country there are asylums for beggars. There are no beggars, there must be none; and there must be no feelings of sympathy, since that would be a confession that beggary existed.

'But he laboured, he gave you enjoyment, he besought you to give him something of your superfluity in payment for his labour of which you took advantage. But you looked on him with a cool smile as on one of the curiosities in your lofty brilliant palaces;

and though there were a hundred of you, favoured with happiness and wealth, not one man or one woman among you gave him a sou. Abashed he went away from you, and the thoughtless throng, laughing, followed and ridiculed not you, but him, because you were cold, harsh, and dishonourable; because you robbed him in receiving the entertainment which he gave you; for this you jeered him.

"On the 19th of July, 1857, in Lucerne, before the Schweitzerhof Hotel, in which were lodging very opulent people, a wandering beggar minstrel sang for half an hour his songs, and played his guitar. About a hundred people listened to him. The minstrel thrice asked all to give him something. No one person gave him a thing, and many made sport of him.'

'This is not an invention, but an actual fact, as those who desire can find out for themselves by consulting the papers for the list of those who were at the schweitzerhof on the 19th of July.

'This is an event which the historians of our time ought to describe in letters of inextinguishable flame. This even is more significant and more serious, and fraught with far deeper meaning, than the facts that are printed in newspapers and histories. That the English have killed several thousand Chinese because the Chinese would not sell them anything for money while their land is overflowing with ringing coins; that the French have killed several thousand Kabyles because the wheat grows well in Africa, and because constant war is essential for the drill of an army; that the Turkish ambassador in Naples must not be a Jew; and that the Emperor Napoleon walks about in Plombières, and gives his people the express assurance that he rules only in direct accordance with the will of the people—all these are words which darken or reveal something long known. But the episode that took place in Lucerne on the 19th of July seems to me something entirely novel and strange, and it is connected not with the everlastingly ugly side of human nature, but with a well-known epoch in the development of society. This fact is not for the history of human activities, but for the history of progress and civilization.

'Why is it that this inhuman fact, impossible in any German, French, or Italian country, is quite possible here where civilization, freedom, and equality are carried to the highest degree of development, where there are gathered together the most civilized travellers from the most civilized nations? Why is it that these people who, in their palaces, their meetings, and their societies, labour warmly for the condition of the celibate Chinese in India, about the spread of Christianity and culture in Africa, about the formation of societies for attaining all perfection,—why is it that they should not find in their souls the simple, primitive feeling of human sympathy? Has such a feeling entirely disappeared, and has its place been taken by vainglory, ambition, and cupidity, governing these men in their palaces, meetings, and societies? Has the spreading of that reasonable, egotistical association of people, which we call civilization, destroyed and rendered nugatory the desire for instinctive and loving association? And is this that boasted equality for which so much innocent blood has been shed, and so many crimes have been perpetrated? Is it possible that nations, like children, can be made happy by the mere sound of the word "equality"?

'Equality before the law? Does the whole life of a people revolve within the sphere of law? Only the thousandth part of it is subject to the law; the rest lies outside of it, in the sphere of the customs and intuitions of society.

'But in society the lackey is better dressed than the minstrel, and insults him with impunity. I am better dressed than the lackey, and insult him with impunity. The Swiss considers me higher, but the minstrel lower, than himself; when I made the minstrel my companion, he felt that he was on an equality with us both, and behaved rudely. I was impudent to the Swiss, and the Swiss acknowledged that he was inferior to me. The waiter was impudent to the minstrel, and the minstrel accepted the fact that he was inferior to the waiter.

'And is that government free, even though men seriously call it free, where a single citizen can be thrown into prison, because, without harming any one, without interfering with any one, he does the only thing he can to prevent himself from dying of starvation?

'A wretched, pitiable creature is man with his craving for positive solutions, thrown into this everlastingly tossing, limitless ocean of good and evil, of facts, of combinations and contradictions. For centuries men have been struggling and laboring to put the good on one side, the evil on the other. Centuries will pass, and no matter how much the unprejudiced mind may strive to decide where the balance lies between the good and the evil, the scales will refuse to tip the beam, and there will always be equal quantities of the good and the evil on each scale.

'If only man would learn to form judgments, and not indulge in rash and arbitrary thoughts, and not to make reply to questions that are propounded merely to remain forever unanswered! If only he would learn that; every thought is both a lie and a truth!—a lie from the one-sidedness and inability of man to recognize all truth; and true because it expresses one side of mortal endeavour. There are divisions in this everlastingly tumultuous, endless, endlessly confused chaos of the good and the evil. They have drawn imaginary lines over this ocean, and they contend that the ocean is really thus divided.

'But are there not millions of other possible subdivisions from absolutely different standpoints, in other planes? Certainly these novel subdivisions will be made in centuries to come, just as millions of different ones have been made in centuries past.

'Civilization is good, barbarism is evil; freedom, good, slavery, evil. Now this imaginary knowledge annihilates the instinctive, beatific, primitive craving for the good which is in human nature.

And who will explain to me what is freedom, what is despotism, what is civilization, what is barbarism?

'Where are the boundaries that separate them? And whose soul possesses so absolute a standard of good and evil as to measure these fleeting, complicated facts? Whose intellect is so great as to comprehend and weigh all the facts in the irretrievable past? And who can find any circumstance in which good and evil do not exist together? And because I know that I see more of one than of the other, is it not because my standpoint is wrong? And who has the ability to separate himself so absolutely from life, even for a moment, as to look upon it independently from above?

'One, only one infallible Guide we have—the universal Spirit which penetrates all collectively and as units, which has endowed each of us with the craving for the right; the Spirit which commands the tree to grow toward the sun, which commands the flower in autumn-tide to scatter its seed, and which commands each one of us unconsciously to draw closer together. And this one unerring, inspiring voice rings out louder than the noisy, hasty development of civilization.

'Who is the greater man, and who the greater barbarian—that lord, who, seeing the minstrel's well-worn clothes, angrily left the table, who gave him not the millionth part of his possessions in payment of his labour, and now lazily sitting in his brilliant, comfortable room, calmly expresses his opinion about the events that are happening in China, and justifies the massacres that have been done there; or the little minstrel, who, risking imprisonment, with a franc in his pocket, and doing no harm to any one, has been going about for a score of years, up hill and down dale, rejoicing men's hearts with his songs, though they have jeered at him, and almost cast him out of the pale of humanity; and who, in weariness and cold and shame, has gone off to sleep, no one knows where, on his filthy straw?'

At this moment, from the city, through the dead silence of the night, far, far away, I caught the sound of the little man's guitar and his voice.

'No,' something involuntarily said to me, 'you have no right to commiserate the little man, or to blame the lord for his well-being. Who can weigh the inner happiness which is found in the soul of each of these men? There he stands somewhere in the muddy road, and gazes at the brilliant moonlit sky, and gayly sings amid the smiling, fragrant night; in his soul there is no reproach, no anger, no regret. And who knows what is transpiring now in the hearts of all these men within those opulent, brilliant rooms? Who knows if they all have as much unencumbered, sweet delight in life, and as much satisfaction with the world, as dwells in the soul of that little man?

'Endless are the mercy and wisdom of Him who has permitted and formed all these contradictions. Only to thee, miserable little worm of the dust, audaciously, lawlessly attempting to fathom His laws, His designs—only to thee do they seem like contradictions.

'Full of love He looks down from His bright, immeasurable height, and rejoices in the endless harmony in which you all move in endless contradictions. In thy pride thou hast thought thyself able to separate thyself from the laws of the universe. No, thou also, with thy petty, ridiculous anger against the waiters,—thou also hast disturbed the harmonious craving for the eternal and the infinite.'

9

THERE ARE NO GUILTY PEOPLE

Mine is a strange and wonderful lot! The chances are that there is not a single wretched beggar suffering under the luxury and oppression of the rich who feels anything like as keenly as I do either the injustice, the cruelty, and the horror of their oppression of and contempt for the poor; or the grinding humiliation and misery which befall the great majority of the workers, the real producers of all that makes life possible. I have felt this for a long time, and as the years have passed by the feeling has grown and grown, until recently it reached its climax. Although I feel all this so vividly, I still live on amid the depravity and sins of rich society; and I cannot leave it, because I have neither the knowledge nor the strength to do so. I cannot. I do not know how to change my life so that my physical needs—food, sleep, clothing, my going to and fro—may be satisfied without a sense of shame and wrongdoing in the position which I fill.

There was a time when I tried to change my position, which was not in harmony with my conscience; but the conditions created by the past, by my family and its claims upon me, were so complicated that they would not let me out of their grasp, or rather, I did not know how to free myself. I had not the strength. Now that I am over eighty and have become feeble, I have given up trying to free myself; and, strange to say, as my feebleness increases

I realize more and more strongly the wrongfulness of my position, and it grows more and more intolerable to me.

It has occurred to me that I do not occupy this position for nothing: that Providence intended that I should lay bare the truth of my feelings, so that I might atone for all that causes my suffering, and might perhaps open the eyes of those—or at least of some of those—who are still blind to what I see so clearly, and thus might lighten the burden of that vast majority who, under existing conditions, are subjected to bodily and spiritual suffering by those who deceive them and also deceive themselves. Indeed, it may be that the position which I occupy gives me special facilities for revealing the artificial and criminal relations which exist between men—for telling the whole truth in regard to that position without confusing the issue by attempting to vindicate myself, and without rousing the envy of the rich and feelings of oppression in the hearts of the poor and downtrodden. I am so placed that I not only have no desire to vindicate myself; but, on the contrary, I find it necessary to make an effort lest I should exaggerate the wickedness of the great among whom I live, of whose society I am ashamed, whose attitude towards their fellow-men I detest with my whole soul, though I find it impossible to separate my lot from theirs. But I must also avoid the error of those democrats and others who, in defending the oppressed and the enslaved, do not see their failings and mistakes, and who do not make sufficient allowance for the difficulties created, the mistakes inherited from the past, which in a degree lessens the responsibility of the upper classes.

Free from desire for self-vindication, free from fear of an emancipated people, free from that envy and hatred which the oppressed feel for their oppressors, I am in the best possible position to see the truth and to tell it. Perhaps that is why Providence placed me in such a position. I will do my best to turn it to account.

Alexander Ivanovich Volgin, a bachelor and a clerk in a

Moscow bank at a salary of eight thousand roubles a year, a man much respected in his own set, was staying in a country-house. His host was a wealthy landowner, owning some twenty-five hundred acres, and had married his guest's cousin. Volgin, tired after an evening spent in playing vint a game of cards similar to auction bridge.] for small stakes with members of the family, went to his room and placed his watch, silver cigarette-case, pocket-book, big leather purse, and pocket-brush and comb on a small table covered with a white cloth, and then, taking off his coat, waistcoat, shirt, trousers, and underclothes, his silk socks and English boots, put on his nightshirt and dressing-gown. His watch pointed to midnight. Volgin smoked a cigarette, lay on his face for about five minutes reviewing the day's impressions; then, blowing out his candle, he turned over on his side and fell asleep about one o'clock, in spite of a good deal of restlessness. Awaking next morning at eight he put on his slippers and dressing-gown, and rang the bell.

The old butler, Stephen, the father of a family and the grandfather of six grandchildren, who had served in that house for thirty years, entered the room hurriedly, with bent legs, carrying in the newly blackened boots which Volgin had taken off the night before, a well-brushed suit, and a clean shirt. The guest thanked him, and then asked what the weather was like (the blinds were drawn so that the sun should not prevent any one from sleeping till eleven o'clock if he were so inclined), and whether his hosts had slept well. He glanced at his watch—it was still early—and began to wash and dress. His water was ready, and everything on the washing-stand and dressing-table was ready for use and properly laid out—his soap, his tooth and hair brushes, his nail scissors and files. He washed his hands and face in a leisurely fashion, cleaned and manicured his nails, pushed back the skin with the towel, and sponged his stout white body from head to foot. Then he began to brush his hair. Standing in front of the mirror, he first brushed his curly beard, which was beginning to turn grey, with two English brushes, parting it down the middle. Then he combed his hair, which was already showing signs of getting thin, with a large tortoise-shell comb. Putting on his underlinen, his socks, his boots, his trousers—which were held up by elegant braces—and his waistcoat, he sat down coatless in an easy chair to rest after dressing, lit a cigarette, and began to think where he should go for a walk that morning—to the park or to Littleports (what a funny name for a wood!). He thought he would go to Littleports.

Then he must answer Simon Nicholaevich's letter; but there was time enough for that. Getting up with an air of resolution, he took out his watch. It was already five minutes to nine. He put his watch into his waistcoat pocket, and his purse—with all that was left of the hundred and eighty roubles he had taken for his journey, and for the incidental expenses of his fortnight's stay with his cousin—and then he placed into his trouser pocket his cigarette-case and electric cigarette-lighter, and two clean handkerchiefs into his coat pockets, and went out of the room, leaving as usual the mess and confusion which he had made to be cleared up by Stephen, an old man of over fifty.

Stephen expected Volgin to 'remunerate' him, as he said, being so accustomed to the work that he did not feel the slightest repugnance for it. Glancing at a mirror, and feeling satisfied with his appearance, Volgin went into the dining room.

There, thanks to the efforts of the housekeeper, the footman, and under-butler—the latter had risen at dawn in order to run home to sharpen his son's scythe—breakfast was ready. On a spotless white cloth stood a boiling, shiny, silver samovar (at least it looked like silver), a coffee-pot, hot milk, cream, butter, and all sorts of fancy white bread and biscuits. The only persons at table were the second son of the house, his tutor (a student), and the secretary. The host, who was an active member of the Zemstvo and a great farmer, had already left the house, having gone at eight o'clock to attend to his work. Volgin, while drinking his coffee, talked to the student and the secretary about the weather, and yesterday's vint, and discussed Theodorite's peculiar behaviour the night before, as he had been very rude to his father without the slightest cause. Theodorite was the grown-up son of the house, and a ne'er-do-well. His name was Theodore, but some one had once called him Theodorite either as a joke or to tease him; and, as it seemed funny, the name stuck to him, although his doings were no longer in the least amusing. So it was now. He had been to the university, but left it in his second year, and joined a regiment of horse guards; but he gave that up also, and was now living in the country, doing nothing, finding fault, and feeling discontented with everything. Theodorite was still in bed: so were the other members of the household—Anna Mikhailovna, its mistress; her sister, the widow of a general; and a landscape painter who lived with the family.

Volgin took his panama hat from the hall table (it had cost twenty roubles) and his cane with its carved ivory handle, and went out. Crossing the veranda, gay with flowers, he walked through the flower garden, in the centre of which was a raised round bed, with rings of red, white, and blue flowers, and the initials of the mistress of the house done in carpet bedding in the centre. Leaving the flower garden Volgin entered the avenue of lime trees, hundreds of years old, which peasant girls were tidying and sweeping with spades and brooms. The gardener was busy measuring, and a boy was bringing something in a cart. Passing these Volgin went into the park of at least 125 acres, filled with fine old trees, and intersected by a network of well-kept walks. Smoking as he strolled Volgin took his favourite path past the summer-house into the fields beyond. It was pleasant in the park, but it was still nicer in the fields. On the right some women who were digging potatoes formed a mass of bright red and white colour; on the left were wheat fields, meadows, and grazing cattle; and in the foreground, slightly to the right, were the dark, dark oaks of Littleports. Volgin took a deep breath, and felt glad that he was alive, especially here in his cousin's home, where he was so thoroughly enjoying the rest from his work at the bank.

'Lucky people to live in the country,' he thought. 'True, what with his farming and his Zemstvo, the owner of the estate has very little peace even in the country, but that is his own lookout.' Volgin shook his head, lit another cigarette, and, stepping out firmly with his powerful feet clad in his thick English boots, began to think of the heavy winter's work in the bank that was in front of him. 'I shall be there every day from ten to two, sometimes even till five. And the board meetings...And private interviews with clients... Then the Duma. Whereas here....It is delightful. It may be a little dull, but it is not for long.'

He smiled. After a stroll in Littleports he turned back, going straight across a fallow field which was being ploughed. A herd of cows, calves, sheep, and pigs, which belonged to the village community, was grazing there. The shortest way to the park was to pass through the herd. He frightened the sheep, which ran away one after another, and were followed by the pigs, of which two little ones stared solemnly at him. The shepherd boy called to the sheep and cracked his whip. 'How far behind Europe we are,' thought Volgin, recalling his frequent holidays abroad. 'You would not find a single cow like that anywhere in Europe.' Then, wanting to find out where the path which branched off from the one he was on led to and who was the owner of the herd, he called to the boy. 'Whose herd is it?' The boy was so filled with wonder, verging on terror, when he gazed at the hat, the well-brushed beard, and above all the gold-rimmed eyeglasses, that he could not reply at once. When Volgin repeated his question the boy pulled himself together, and said, 'Ours.' 'But whose is "ours"?' said Volgin, shaking his head and smiling. The boy was wearing shoes of plaited birch bark, bands of linen round his legs, a dirty, unbleached shirt ragged at the shoulder, and a cap the peak of which had been torn.

'Whose is "ours"?'

'The Pirogov village herd.'

'How old are you?'

'I don't know.'

'Can you read?'

'No, I can't.'

'Didn't you go to school?'

'Yes, I did.'

'Couldn't you learn to read?'

'No.'

'Where does that path lead?'

The boy told him, and Volgin went on towards the house, thinking how he would chaff Nicholas Petrovich about the deplorable condition of the village schools in spite of all his efforts.

On approaching the house Volgin looked at his watch, and saw that it was already past eleven. He remembered that Nicholas Petrovich was going to drive to the nearest town, and that he had meant to give him a letter to post to Moscow; but the letter was not written. The letter was a very important one to a friend, asking him to bid for him for a picture of the Madonna which was to be offered for sale at an auction. As he reached the house he saw at the door four big, well-fed, well-groomed, thoroughbred horses harnessed to a carriage, the black lacquer of which glistened in the sun. The coachman was seated on the box in a kaftan, with a silver belt, and the horses were jingling their silver bells from time to time.

A bare-headed, barefooted peasant in a ragged kaftan stood at the front door. He bowed. Volgin asked what he wanted.

'I have come to see Nicholas Petrovich.'

'What about?'

'Because I am in distress—my horse has died.'

Volgin began to question him. The peasant told him how he

was situated.

He had five children, and this had been his only horse. Now it was gone.

He wept.

'What are you going to do?'

'To beg.' And he knelt down, and remained kneeling in spite of Volgin's expostulations.

'What is your name?'

'Mitri Sudarikov,' answered the peasant, still kneeling.

Volgin took three roubles from his purse and gave them to the peasant, who showed his gratitude by touching the ground with his forehead, and then went into the house. His host was standing in the hall.

'Where is your letter?' he asked, approaching Volgin; 'I am just off.'

'I'm awfully sorry, I'll write it this minute, if you will let me. I forgot all about it. It's so pleasant here that one can forget anything.'

'All right, but do be quick. The horses have already been standing a quarter of an hour, and the flies are biting viciously. Can you wait, Arsenty?' he asked the coachman.

'Why not?' said the coachman, thinking to himself, 'why do they order the horses when they aren't ready? The rush the grooms and I had—just to stand here and feed the flies.'

'Directly, directly,' Volgin went towards his room, but turned back to ask Nicholas Petrovich about the begging peasant.

'Did you see him?—He's a drunkard, but still he is to be pitied. Do be quick!'

Volgin got out his case, with all the requisites for writing, wrote the letter, made out a cheque for a hundred and eighty roubles, and, sealing down the envelope, took it to Nicholas Petrovich.

'Goodbye.'

Volgin read the newspapers till luncheon. He only read the Liberal papers: *The Russian Gazette*, *Speech*, sometimes *The Russian Word*—but he would not touch The New Times, to which his host subscribed.

While he was scanning at his ease the political news, the Tsar's doings, the doings of President, and ministers and decisions in the Duma, and was just about to pass on to the general news, theatres, science, murders and cholera, he heard the luncheon bell ring.

Thanks to the efforts of upwards of ten human beings—counting laundresses, gardeners, cooks, kitchen-maids, butlers and footmen—the table was sumptuously laid for eight, with silver waterjugs, decanters, kvass, wine, mineral waters, cut glass, and fine table linen, while two men-servants were continually hurrying to and fro, bringing in and serving, and then clearing away the hors d'oeuvre and the various hot and cold courses.

The hostess talked incessantly about everything that she had been doing, thinking, and saying; and she evidently considered that everything that she thought, said, or did was perfect, and that it would please every one except those who were fools. Volgin felt and knew that everything she said was stupid, but it would never do to let it be seen, and so he kept up the conversation. Theodorite was glum and silent; the student occasionally exchanged a few words with the widow. Now and again there was a pause in the conversation, and then Theodorite interposed, and every one became miserably depressed. At such moments the hostess ordered some dish that had not been served, and the footman hurried off to the kitchen, or to the housekeeper, and hurried back again. Nobody felt inclined either to talk or to eat. But they all forced themselves to eat and to talk, and so luncheon went on.

The peasant who had been begging because his horse had died was named Mitri Sudarikov. He had spent the whole day before he went to the squire over his dead horse. First of all he went to the knacker, Sanin, who lived in a village near. The knacker was out, but he waited for him, and it was dinner-time when he had finished bargaining over the price of the skin. Then he borrowed a neighbour's horse to take his own to a field to be buried, as it is forbidden to bury dead animals near a village.

Adrian would not lend his horse because he was getting in his potatoes, but Stephen took pity on Mitri and gave way to his persuasion. He even lent a hand in lifting the dead horse into the cart. Mitri tore off the shoes from the forelegs and gave them to his wife. One was broken, but the other one was whole. While he was digging the grave with a spade which was very blunt, the knacker appeared and took off the skin; and the carcass was then thrown into the hole and covered up. Mitri felt tired, and went into Matrena's hut, where he drank half a bottle of vodka with Sanin to console himself. Then he went home, quarrelled with his wife, and lay down to sleep on the hay. He did not undress, but slept just as he was, with a ragged coat for a coverlet. His wife was in the hut with the girls—there were four of them, and the youngest was only five weeks old. Mitri woke up before dawn as usual. He groaned as the memory of the day before broke in upon him—how the horse had struggled and struggled, and then fallen down. Now there was no horse, and all he had was the price of the skin, four roubles and eighty kopeks. Getting up he arranged the linen bands on his legs, and went through the yard into the hut. His wife was putting straw into the stove with one hand, with the other she was holding a baby girl to her breast, which was hanging out of her dirty chemise.

Mitri crossed himself three times, turning towards the corner in which the ikons hung, and repeated some utterly meaningless words, which he called prayers, to the Trinity and the Virgin, the Creed and our Father.

'Isn't there any water?'

'The girl's gone for it. I've got some tea. Will you go up to the squire?'

'Yes, I'd better.' The smoke from the stove made him cough.

He took a rag off the wooden bench and went into the porch. The girl had just come back with the water. Mitri filled his mouth with water from the pail and squirted it out on his hands, took some more in his mouth to wash his face, dried himself with the rag, then parted and smoothed his curly hair with his fingers and went out. A little girl of about ten, with nothing on but a dirty shirt, came towards him. 'Good-morning, Uncle Mitri,' she said; 'you are to come and thrash.'

'All right, I'll come,' replied Mitri. He understood that he was expected to return the help given the week before by Kumushkir, a man as poor as he was himself, when he was thrashing his own corn with a horse-driven machine. 'Tell them I'll come—I'll come at lunch time. I've got to go to Ugrumi.' Mitri went back to the hut, and changing his birch-bark shoes and the linen bands on his legs, started off to see the squire. After he had got three roubles from Volgin, and the same sum from Nicholas Petrovich, he returned to his house, gave the money to his wife, and went to his neighbour's. The thrashing machine was humming, and the driver was shouting. The lean horses were going slowly round him, straining at their traces. The driver was shouting to them in a monotone, 'Now, there, my dears.' Some women were unbinding sheaves, others were raking up the scattered straw and ears, and others again were gathering great armfuls of corn and handing them to the men to feed the machine. The work was in full swing. In the kitchen garden, which Mitri had to pass, a girl, clad only in a long shirt, was digging potatoes which she put into a basket.

'Where's your grandfather?' asked Mitri. 'He's in the barn.' Mitri went to the barn and set to work at once. The old man of eighty knew of Mitri's trouble. After greeting him, he gave him his place to feed the machine.

Mitri took off his ragged coat, laid it out of the way near the fence, and then began to work vigorously, raking the corn together and throwing it into the machine. The work went on without interruption until the dinner-hour. The cocks had crowed two or three times, but no one paid any attention to them; not because the workers did not believe them, but because they were scarcely heard for the noise of the work and the talk about it. At last the whistle of the squire's steam thrasher sounded three miles away, and then the owner came into the barn. He was a straight old man of eighty. 'It's time to stop,' he said; 'it's dinner-time.' Those at work seemed to redouble their efforts. In a moment the straw was cleared away; the grain that had been thrashed was separated from the chaff and brought in, and then the workers went into the hut.

The hut was smoke-begrimed, as its stove had no chimney, but it had been tidied up, and benches stood round the table, making room for all those who had been working, of whom there were nine, not counting the owners.

Bread, soup, boiled potatoes, and kvass were placed on the table.

An old one-armed beggar, with a bag slung over his shoulder, came in with a crutch during the meal.

'Peace be to this house. A good appetite to you. For Christ's sake give me something.'

'God will give it to you,' said the mistress, already an old woman, and the daughter-in-law of the master. 'Don't be angry with us.' An old man, who was still standing near the door, said, 'Give him some bread, Martha. How can you?'

'I am only wondering whether we shall have enough.'

'Oh, it is wrong, Martha. God tells us to help the poor. Cut him a slice.'

Martha obeyed. The beggar went away. The man in charge of the thrashing-machine got up, said grace, thanked his hosts, and went away to rest.

Mitri did not lie down, but ran to the shop to buy some tobacco. He was longing for a smoke. While he smoked he chatted to a man from Demensk, asking the price of cattle, as he saw that he would not be able to manage without selling a cow. When he returned to the others, they were already back at work again; and so it went on till the evening.

Among these downtrodden, duped, and defrauded men, who are becoming demoralized by overwork, and being gradually done to death by underfeeding, there are men living who consider themselves Christians; and others so enlightened that they feel no further need for Christianity or for any religion, so superior do they appear in their own esteem. And yet their hideous, lazy lives are supported by the degrading, excessive labour of these slaves, not to mention the labour of millions of other slaves, toiling in factories to produce samovars, silver, carriages, machines, and the like for their use. They live among these horrors, seeing them and yet not seeing them, although often kind at heart—old men and women, young men and maidens, mothers and children—poor children who are being vitiated and trained into moral blindness.

Here is a bachelor grown old, the owner of thousands of acres, who has lived a life of idleness, greed, and over-indulgence, who reads *The New Times*, and is astonished that the government can be so unwise as to permit Jews to enter the university. There is his guest, formerly the governor of a province, now a senator with a big salary, who reads with satisfaction that a congress of lawyers has passed a resolution in favour of capital punishment. Their political enemy, N. P., reads a liberal paper, and cannot understand the blindness of the government in allowing the union of Russian men to exist.

Here is a kind, gentle mother of a little girl reading a story to her about Fox, a dog that lamed some rabbits. And here is this little girl.

During her walks she sees other children, barefooted, hungry, hunting for green apples that have fallen from the trees; and, so accustomed is she to the sight, that these children do not seem to her to be children such as she is, but only part of the usual surroundings—the familiar landscape.

Why is this?

10

GOD SEES THE TRUTH, BUT WAITS

In the town of Vladimir lived a young merchant named Ivan Dmitrich Aksionov. He had two shops and a house of his own.

Aksionov was a handsome, fair-haired, curly-headed fellow, full of fun, and very fond of singing. When quite a young man he had been given to drink, and was riotous when he had had too much; but after he married he gave up drinking, except now and then.

One summer Aksionov was going to the Nizhny Fair, and as he bade goodbye to his family, his wife said to him, 'Ivan Dmitrich, do not start today; I have had a bad dream about you.'

Aksionov laughed, and said, 'You are afraid that when I get to the fair I shall go on a spree.'

His wife replied: 'I do not know what I am afraid of; all I know is that I had a bad dream. I dreamt you returned from the town, and when you took off your cap I saw that your hair was quite grey.'

Aksionov laughed. 'That's a lucky sign,' said he. 'See if I don't sell out all my goods, and bring you some presents from the fair.'

So he said goodbye to his family, and drove away.

When he had travelled half-way, he met a merchant whom he knew, and they put up at the same inn for the night. They had some tea together, and then went to bed in adjoining rooms.

It was not Aksionov's habit to sleep late, and, wishing to travel while it was still cool, he aroused his driver before dawn, and told him to put in the horses.

Then he made his way across to the landlord of the inn (who lived in a cottage at the back), paid his bill, and continued his journey.

When he had gone about twenty-five miles, he stopped for the horses to be fed. Aksionov rested awhile in the passage of the inn, then he stepped out into the porch, and, ordering a samovar to be heated, got out his guitar and began to play.

Suddenly a troika drove up with tinkling bells and an official alighted, followed by two soldiers. He came to Aksionov and began to question him, asking him who he was and whence he came. Aksionov answered him fully, and said, 'Won't you have some tea with me?' But the official went on cross-questioning him and asking him. 'Where did you spend last night? Were you alone, or with a fellow-merchant? Did you see the other merchant this morning? Why did you leave the inn before dawn?'

Aksionov wondered why he was asked all these questions, but he described all that had happened, and then added, 'Why do you cross-question me as if I were a thief or a robber? I am travelling on business of my own, and there is no need to question me.'

Then the official, calling the soldiers, said, 'I am the police-officer of this district, and I question you because the merchant with whom you spent last night has been found with his throat cut. We must search your things.'

They entered the house. The soldiers and the police-officer unstrapped Aksionov's luggage and searched it. Suddenly the officer drew a knife out of a bag, crying, 'Whose knife is this?'

Aksionov looked, and seeing a blood-stained knife taken from his bag, he was frightened.

'How is it there is blood on this knife?'

Aksionov tried to answer, but could hardly utter a word, and only stammered: 'I—don't know—not mine.' Then the police-officer said: 'This morning the merchant was found in bed with his throat cut. You are the only person who could have done it. The house was locked from inside, and no one else was there. Here is this blood-stained knife in your bag and your face and manner betray you! Tell me how you killed him, and how much money you stole?'

Aksionov swore he had not done it; that he had not seen the merchant after they had had tea together; that he had no money except eight thousand rubles of his own, and that the knife was not his. But his voice was broken, his face pale, and he trembled with fear as though he were guilty.

The police-officer ordered the soldiers to bind Aksionov and to put him in the cart. As they tied his feet together and flung him into the cart, Aksionov crossed himself and wept. His money and goods were taken from him, and he was sent to the nearest town and imprisoned there. Enquiries as to his character were made in Vladimir. The merchants and other inhabitants of that town said that in former days he used to drink and waste his time, but that he was a good man. Then the trial came on: he was charged with murdering a merchant from Ryazan, and robbing him of twenty thousand rubles.

His wife was in despair, and did not know what to believe. Her children were all quite small; one was a baby at her breast. Taking them all with her, she went to the town where her husband was in jail. At first she was not allowed to see him; but after much begging, she obtained permission from the officials, and was taken to him. When she saw her husband in prison-dress and in chains, shut up with thieves and criminals, she fell down, and did not come to her senses for a long time. Then she drew her children to her, and sat down near him. She told him of things at home, and asked about what had happened to him. He told her all, and she asked, 'What can we do now?'

'We must petition the Czar not to let an innocent man perish.'

His wife told him that she had sent a petition to the Czar, but it had not been accepted.

Aksionov did not reply, but only looked downcast.

Then his wife said, 'It was not for nothing I dreamt your hair had turned grey. You remember? You should not have started that day.' And passing her fingers through his hair, she said: 'Vanya dearest, tell your wife the truth; was it not you who did it?'

'So you, too, suspect me!' said Aksionov, and, hiding his face in his hands, he began to weep. Then a soldier came to say that the wife and children must go away; and Aksionov said good-bye to his family for the last time.

When they were gone, Aksionov recalled what had been said, and when he remembered that his wife also had suspected him, he said to himself, 'It seems that only God can know the truth; it is to Him alone we must appeal, and from Him alone expect mercy.'

And Aksionov wrote no more petitions; gave up all hope, and only prayed to God.

Aksionov was condemned to be flogged and sent to the mines. So he was flogged with a knot, and when the wounds made by the knot were healed, he was driven to Siberia with other convicts.

For twenty-six years Aksionov lived as a convict in Siberia. His hair turned white as snow, and his beard grew long, thin, and grey. All his mirth went; he stooped; he walked slowly, spoke little, and never laughed, but he often prayed.

In prison Aksionov learnt to make boots, and earned a little money, with which he bought The Lives of the Saints. He read this book when there was light enough in the prison; and on Sundays in the prison-church he read the lessons and sang in the choir; for his voice was still good.

The prison authorities liked Aksionov for his meekness, and his fellow-prisoners respected him: they called him 'Grandfather,' and 'The Saint.' When they wanted to petition the prison authorities about anything, they always made Aksionov their spokesman, and when there were quarrels among the prisoners they came to him to put things right, and to judge the matter.

No news reached Aksionov from his home, and he did not even know if his wife and children were still alive.

One day a fresh gang of convicts came to the prison. In the evening the old prisoners collected round the new ones and asked them what towns or villages they came from, and what they were sentenced for. Among the rest Aksionov sat down near the newcomers, and listened with downcast air to what was said.

One of the new convicts, a tall, strong man of sixty, with a closely-cropped grey beard, was telling the others what be had been arrested for.

'Well, friends,' he said, 'I only took a horse that was tied to a sledge, and I was arrested and accused of stealing. I said I had only taken it to get home quicker, and had then let it go; besides, the driver was a personal friend of mine. So I said, "It's all right." "No," said they, "you stole it." But how or where I stole it they could not say. I once really did something wrong, and ought by rights to have come here long ago, but that time I was not found out. Now I have been sent here for nothing at all...Eh, but it's lies I'm telling you; I've been to Siberia before, but I did not stay long.'

'Where are you from?' asked some one.

'From Vladimir. My family are of that town. My name is Makar, and they also call me Semyonich.'

Aksionov raised his head and said: 'Tell me, Semyonich, do you know anything of the merchants Aksionov of Vladimir? Are they still alive?'

'Know them? Of course I do. The Aksionovs are rich, though their father is in Siberia: a sinner like ourselves, it seems! As for you, Gran'dad, how did you come here?'

Aksionov did not like to speak of his misfortune. He only sighed, and said, 'For my sins I have been in prison these twenty-six years.'

'What sins?' asked Makar Semyonich.

But Aksionov only said, 'Well, well—I must have deserved it!' He would have said no more, but his companions told the newcomers how Aksionov came to be in Siberia; how someone had killed a merchant, and had put the knife among Aksionov's things, and Aksionov had been unjustly condemned.

When Makar Semyonich heard this, he looked at Aksionov, slapped his own knee, and exclaimed, 'Well, this is wonderful! Really wonderful! But how old you've grown, Gran'dad!'

The others asked him why he was so surprised, and where he had seen Aksionov before; but Makar Semyonich did not reply. He only said: 'It's wonderful that we should meet here, lads!'

These words made Aksionov wonder whether this man knew who had killed the merchant; so he said, 'Perhaps, Semyonich, you have heard of that affair, or maybe you've seen me before?'

'How could I help hearing? The world's full of rumours. But it's a long time ago, and I've forgotten what I heard.'

'Perhaps you heard who killed the merchant?' asked Aksionov.

Makar Semyonich laughed, and replied: 'It must have been him in whose bag the knife was found! If someone else hid the knife there, "He's not a thief till he's caught," as the saying is. How could any one put a knife into your bag while it was under your head? It would surely have woke you up.'

When Aksionov heard these words, he felt sure this was the man who had killed the merchant. He rose and went away. All that night Aksionov lay awake. He felt terribly unhappy, and all sorts of images rose in his mind. There was the image of his wife as she was when he parted from her to go to the fair. He saw her as if she were present; her face and her eyes rose before him; he heard her speak and laugh. Then he saw his children, quite little, as they were at that time: one with a little cloak on, another at his mother's breast. And then he remembered himself as he used to be—young and merry. He remembered how he sat playing the guitar in the porch of the inn where he was arrested, and how free from care he had been. He saw, in his mind, the place where he was flogged, the executioner, and the people standing around; the chains, the convicts, all the twenty-six years of his prison life, and his premature old age. The thought of it all made him so wretched that he was ready to kill himself.

'And it's all that villain's doing!' thought Aksionov. And his anger was so great against Makar Semyonich that he longed for vengeance, even if he himself should perish for it. He kept repeating prayers all night, but could get no peace. During the day he did not go near Makar Semyonich, nor even look at him.

A fortnight passed in this way. Aksionov could not sleep at night, and was so miserable that he did not know what to do.

One night as he was walking about the prison he noticed some earth that came rolling out from under one of the shelves on which the prisoners slept. He stopped to see what it was. Suddenly Makar Semyonich crept out from under the shelf, and looked up at Aksionov with frightened face. Aksionov tried to pass without looking at him, but Makar seized his hand and told him that he had dug a hole under the wall, getting rid of the earth by putting it into his high-boots, and emptying it out every day on the road when the prisoners were driven to their work.

'Just you keep quiet, old man, and you shall get out too. If you blab, they'll flog the life out of me, but I will kill you first.'

Aksionov trembled with anger as he looked at his enemy. He drew his hand away, saying, 'I have no wish to escape, and you have no need to kill me; you killed me long ago! As to telling of you—I may do so or not, as God shall direct.'

Next day, when the convicts were led out to work, the convoy soldiers noticed that one or other of the prisoners emptied some earth out of his boots. The prison was searched and the tunnel found. The Governor came and questioned all the prisoners to find out who had dug the hole. They all denied any knowledge of it. Those who knew would not betray Makar Semyonich, knowing he would be flogged almost to death. At last the Governor turned to Aksionov whom he knew to be a just man, and said:

'You are a truthful old man; tell me, before God, who dug the hole?'

Makar Semyonich stood as if he were quite unconcerned, looking at the Governor and not so much as glancing at Aksionov. Aksionov's lips and hands trembled, and for a long time he could not utter a word. He thought, 'Why should I screen him who ruined my life? Let him pay for what I have suffered. But if I tell, they will probably flog the life out of him, and maybe I suspect him wrongly. And, after all, what good would it be to me?'

'Well, old man,' repeated the Governor, 'tell me the truth: who has been digging under the wall?'

Aksionov glanced at Makar Semyonich, and said, 'I cannot say, your honour. It is not God's will that I should tell! Do what you like with me; I am in your hands.'

However much the Governor tried, Aksionov would say no more, and so the matter had to be left.

That night, when Aksionov was lying on his bed and just beginning to doze, some one came quietly and sat down on his bed. He peered through the darkness and recognized Makar.

'What more do you want of me?' asked Aksionov. 'Why have you come here?'

Makar Semyonich was silent. So Aksionov sat up and said, 'What do you want? Go away, or I will call the guard!'

Makar Semyonich bent close over Aksionov, and whispered, 'Ivan Dmitrich, forgive me!'

'What for?' asked Aksionov.

'It was I who killed the merchant and hid the knife among your things. I meant to kill you too, but I heard a noise outside, so I hid the knife in your bag and escaped out of the window.'

Aksionov was silent, and did not know what to say. Makar Semyonich slid off the bed-shelf and knelt upon the ground. 'Ivan Dmitrich,' said he, 'forgive me! For the love of God, forgive me! I will confess that it was I who killed the merchant, and you will be released and can go to your home.'

'It is easy for you to talk,' said Aksionov, 'but I have suffered for you these twenty-six years. Where could I go to now?...My wife is dead, and my children have forgotten me. I have nowhere to go...'

Makar Semyonich did not rise, but beat his head on the floor. 'Ivan Dmitrich, forgive me!' he cried. 'When they flogged me with the knot it was not so hard to bear as it is to see you now...yet you had pity on me, and did not tell. For Christ's sake forgive me, wretch that I am!' And he began to sob.

When Aksionov heard him sobbing he, too, began to weep. 'God will forgive you!' said he. 'Maybe I am a hundred times worse than you.' And at these words his heart grew light, and the longing for home left him. He no longer had any desire to leave the prison, but only hoped for his last hour to come.

In spite of what Aksionov had said, Makar Semyonich confessed his guilt. But when the order for his release came, Aksionov was already dead.

ABOUT TERRY O'BRIEN

Terry O'Brien is an academic with three decades of experience in teaching language and communication skills in India and abroad. He also headed a college under the auspices of the University of Delhi.

A prolific writer, with several books to his credit, Terry O'Brien is a reputed professional motivational speaker and a quizmaster.